W9-BBC-605

DISCARD

FIGHTING
BLOOD

Center Point
Large Print

**This Large Print Book carries the
Seal of Approval of N.A.V.H.**

FIGHTING BLOOD

A Red Clark Western Novel

Gordon Young

Schmaling Mem. Pub. Library
501 Tenth Avenue
Fulton, IL 61252

CENTER POINT LARGE PRINT
THORNDIKE, MAINE

This Center Point Large Print edition
is published in the year 2017 by arrangement with
Golden West Literary Agency.

Copyright © 1932 by Gordon Young.
Copyright © 1932 by Gordon Ray Young
in the British Commonwealth.

First US edition: Doubleday, Doran
First UK edition: Methuen

All rights reserved.

The text of this Large Print edition is unabridged.
In other aspects, this book may vary
from the original edition.
Printed in the United States of America
on permanent paper.
Set in 16-point Times New Roman type.

ISBN: 978-1-68324-352-6 (hardcover)
ISBN: 978-1-68324-356-4 (paperback)

Library of Congress Cataloging-in-Publication Data

Names: Young, Gordon, 1886–1948, author.
Title: Fighting blood : a Red Clark western novel / Gordon Young.
Description: Center Point Large Print edition. | Thorndike, Maine :
Center Point Large Print, 2017.
Identifiers: LCCN 2016059624| ISBN 9781683243526 (hardcover : alk.
paper) | ISBN 9781683243564 (pbk. : alk. paper)
Subjects: LCSH: Large type books. | GSAFD: Western stories.
Classification: LCC PS3547.O4756 F54 2017 | DDC 813/.52—dc23
LC record available at https://lccn.loc.gov/2016059624

CHAPTER 1.

Old Buck Wanders In

As young Red Clark stepped into the lamplight of the wide-open Cross Bar Saloon doorway, a rangy, broad-shouldered man with solemn eyes and drooping mustache was coming out.

The sad, solemn-faced man stopped short, fixing his eyes in a steady, startled stare.

"My gosh! You, Red?"

"Yeah. Leastwise I'd bet so," said Red, putting out his hand. "Why was you asking in that I-seen-a-ghost sort of voice, Buck? Hunh?"

"My gosh! I was just thinking about you, Red. And I didn't have no suspicion you was in a thousand miles of Tajola. Plumb queer."

"You still look natural, Buck. Still look like you'd been hired to enjoy folks's funerals."

"Don't be sarcastic. Let's get over here in the shadows where we can talk." He pulled lightly at Red's arm and they stepped inside. "Makes me feel sort of superspicious, meeting you thisaway. What you doing down here?"

"Folks say jobs is plentiful."

"But a terrible country, Red. That is, for a peaceable man like me."

5

"Yeah, you're peaceable like a drunk Injun off the reservation, you are."

"I'm misunderstood. That's all."

"You're sure easy misunderstood thataway." Red knew that this sad, slow, solemn old Buck Waxman was one of the most unscarable human beings that ever squinted through smoke. "You and me, Buck, once we waded knee deep and barefoot through a little hell fire, didn't we? And if I recollect right, you toted me on your shoulder, part way."

"You don't recollect worth a damn. I like peace and quiet."

"Then what are *you* doing, Buck, down in this hell-raising Tajola country?"

"Me, son, I'm using my gentle influence."

"You ain't got none."

"Red! That ain't a nice way for to talk. I don't want to be down here in Tajola, but I can't help myself. My brother Bill, he's been old Monroe's foreman for near twenty years, so me—"

"You a friend of old Monroe's, Buck?"

"He ain't got no friends, Red. He's just got a payroll."

"Shucks! No man gets you to ride for him if you don't like him."

"I ride for my brother. He's pretty near what you'd call a friend to old Monroe, though folks wonder why. Now me, I try to be always what folks call the innocent bystander."

"Yeah, I know. You stand by a fellow till pigs sprout wings, whether he's innocent or not."

"Today," said old Buck, "I come to town for some grub, the sort you pour out of a bottle. I've been loafing here." With a backhanded lift of thumb across shoulder, he added, "Whale of a poker game going on in there. That's what made me think of you. Young red-headed kid in there losing dollars like they was wormy beans."

"If he's losing, that's sure like me."

"Yessir. About your age. 'Minded me of you. How'd you come to be here, Red?"

"Followed my nose."

"Smelt trouble, huh?" Old Buck shook his head reproachfully. "When did you come to town?"

" 'Bout an hour ago. Got me a room, had some supper, and walked out to see the sights."

"And of course, sorta by instinct, you make a bee line for the Cross Bar Saloon. Careful folks don't hang around here much." Waxman shook his head warningly and added in a lower tone, "Man named Hamel owns the Cross Bar. Owns this here town of Tajola, too. Owns the sheriff. Owns the Cross Bar outfit. And he owns all the lumber there is in town to make coffins with."

"You rouse my curiosity."

"Now me, I got to go up the street a piece to see a fellow. Wanta come along and keep in good company?"

"I'll wait."

"Then go along in and watch that poker game. That young fellow that made me think of you is likely to come out without no pants on. I'll be back pronto. You need my restraining influence, Red."

"Yeah. You and bad whisky, they keep me from going to sleep in church and suchlike unmannerly doings."

Waxman gazed at him with mournful reproach. "That ain't no nice way to talk to an old man," he said.

"You ain't no nice old man for a modest, blushing boy like me to talk to, neither."

Old Buck Waxman shook his head sadly. "I can just see that you're itching to be scratched by trouble. I'll be right back, pronto. Then you and me can have a talk."

He went off with a kind of hasty shambling, loose-jointed, sort of humble and lonesome-like. Red peered after him, grinning.

"Yessir," said Red to himself, "he's a queer old codger. Sees a lot and says nothing much. And folks that take him for a fool would step on a rattlesnake, barefoot. That there slow, sad manner of his has coaxed a lot of bad men to get themselves buried. When old Buck's wandering 'round the range, looking sort of lonesome and half lost, he's up to something."

CHAPTER 2.

Red Trims Some Trimmers

Near the back end of the bar a lamp was hung high so as to cast a funnel-shaped glow of yellow light down on the table where tall stacks of chips, much gold coin, and a sprinkling of silver lay at the elbows of the players.

Red edged into the group that stood about the table and by slow squirming got into a good position to look on.

Six men were playing, four of them in shirt sleeves. Two were gamblers, pale-faced fellows with slender white fingers, and they wore their coats though the room was hot. One of the gamblers was middle-aged, with some gray hairs, but a black curled mustache, greasily waxed. He wore good clothes, and there was a gold watch chain, with a heavy charm dangling, on his vest. He wore rings that seemed to be set with diamonds. Anybody could tell that he thought himself handsome. The other gambler was young, lean, with low-lidded dark eyes, thin mouth, and long, supple fingers.

Red eyed the gamblers with instinctive dislike. He, the son of a famous sheriff, had almost from babyhood learned a lot of things about gunmen, gamblers, rustlers; and he was recklessly unafraid of any and all dishonest men, just as his father, the sheriff, had been.

Two of the other players were full-grown cowboys, men rather; the sort, Red felt after a long, shrewd stare, he wouldn't care to have for friends.

He guessed at once that the man who was banking this game was Hamel, the Cross Bar owner—owner, too, of the lumber from which all coffins were made. Hamel was a big, dark, heavy man with lumpy jaws, something of a belly, and hard eyes. He looked well fed and cruel, tricky, self-confident, but after the manner of saloon keepers, he tried to appear affable and jolly.

Red stared with the most interest at the young fellow who had put Buck Waxman in mind of Red himself. There was actually very little resemblance. Red was lanky, loose-jointed, limber as rawhide. He had a wide mouth and a long nose, and dark freckles were baked in under the sunburn. For all of Red's youth, there was something about him that made people know he was a man, fit for a man's work, and that he was none the less dangerous because he grinned, spoke softly, never got excited. His hair was the color of burned brick. He wore two guns and no gloves.

Red eyed this other boy critically and not unfavorably. A cowboy, too, but with somehow the taint of the East about him and none of Red

Clark's rawhide sinewy strength and quickness. A nice-looking boy, but his face hadn't been whipped by windstorms, scorched by the sun; and he didn't have the muscular gauntness of one who had ridden through stampedes or followed the trail of men who would kill him on sight. But Red was instinctively partial toward him, noticing that he played without nervousness and lost as if it didn't matter. And he was sure in bad company.

It happened that Red's feeling toward professional gamblers was just about the same as his feeling toward any other sort of sneak thieves. He had backed outlaws up against the wall and felt a certain respect for them. He had come down on rustlers with the smoke of burned hair still in their noses and sometimes felt that they were good men who had straggled off the trail. He had once even cut down a horse thief and stood fast, with both guns out, talking for the man's life, though there was no doubt about his guilt. But the sight of sleek, lily-fingered gamblers clawing in chips gave Red much the same sort of sensation that a right-minded dog feels at the sight of a cat.

These gamblers held their cards low down, though well in sight, with both hands up close to their chests, barely skinning the pips as if afraid somebody might spy over their shoulders and signal. Red was pretty sure of what they were doing, because he had seen men examining the bodies of gamblers who had died suddenly in the midst of a game, and he had heard old-timers talk. But these fellows were clever and careful.

The two cowmen, one called Jack Harris, the other Frank Sterns, were ill-natured losers. They slammed the cards about and cursed their luck, as, Red felt, they would no doubt have cussed their wives. Yet they seemed to have unlimited credit. One and then the other would thrust out his paw toward Hamel and say, "Let me have another stack, will you, George?"

The fat, dark, bulky George Hamel would count out a stack of chips, hand it over, then make a notation on a card that he took from his vest pocket.

"Hmm," Red said to himself, "Hamel's staking them pikers and lettin' them lose their shirt tails. He must be a worse judge of character than me, which most saloon keepers ain't, to hand over money thataway. They ain't the sort as pays back what they borrow. Something queer."

Red also thought there was something queer about a boy near his own age having as much money as this young fellow had and losing it so carelessly.

"He looks honest, but I don't suspicion that he's ever mixed much brow sweat with his flapjacks. One thing's sure, the which being that he ain't much educated to the way of a couple of tinhorns with a sucker."

The young fellow bet heavily and lost frequently

but seemed pleased if he stole a pot, as he did now and then, on a pair of deuces or worse.

Then came the time when the younger gambler—he with the lean, pale face, and the long, agile fingers—dealt. The young man sat under the gun, and, his ante being raised by Hamel on the left and seen by all players, he lifted it back with a couple of blues. Sterns came in for the boost; then the second gambler, the middle-aged one with the sleek, well-fed face, gave a wallop of six blues. The dealer pitched away his hand. The young fellow then saw all rises and topped it off with ten blues.

"Whew," said Hamel. "This lets me out."

"I never seen such luck," Harris grumbled and slammed his cards to the table, throwing them away.

"I'm out," Sterns growled.

The big gambler squinted at his hand and murmured, "Nothing much to stay on myself, but if I catch—"

"Cards?" said Wolf Face, the dealer.

The young man shook his head, laid down his hand and covered it with a chip.

"Hell," said Hamel, trying to be pleasant. "Pat hand. Well, it's sure better to be born lucky than handsome—like me."

Bystanders laughed a little.

The big gambler gazed intently at the young fellow as if trying to read his face, then slowly threw away one card and lifted a finger. He took up the card that fell to him, slipped it into his hand, cautiously peeked at the pip, and nodded. "Do your talking."

The young man poked in twenty blues and picked up his cigarette. His fingers were not trembling, and his blue-eyed glance at the gambler was calm. Red Clark, a watchful boy, said to himself, "Good leather!"

The gambler eyed the young fellow with studied deliberation, hesitated, then leaned forward, estimating the table stakes.

"I'll call," said the gambler. He added, "And tap you!"

Men about the table whistled in interested surprise, and bystanders peered at one another with vague head shakes.

The count of the young fellow's chips came to something over twelve hundred. He pushed them in, then spread his cards—a full house, three kings and a pair of sixes.

"Ow," said Hamel, "he did have 'em."

Bystanders clucked commendingly. Folks sort of liked the young fellow's easy manner and steady fingers. Time and again he had bluffed the gamblers out of medium-sized pots and now in a big hand he had the cards.

The boy put out his hand and began to scrape in the pot.

"Just a minute," said the gambler with sinister

softness. "I got something I'd like you to see."

One by one the gambler began to toss his cards to the table. Four deuces fell with noiseless flutter.

"Had 'em all the time," said the gambler, smiling coldly.

The young man gazed at them, then leaned back and said quietly, "All right. I'm through. Five thousand. But that's poker!"

"He's sure a good sport," Hamel announced loudly with unctuous approval.

"Dead game," said the big gambler. "I like thoroughbreds—yeah!" With unhurried movements of soft white hand he began to pick up the chips.

Then there was a hasty stir among the bystanders, gasps and blurted oaths. The gambler looked up sharply with a flicker of fright on his face. He was staring into two guns, and behind them a face that was sun-blackened, bony, muscled at the jaws. It wore a twisted smile, and the blue eyes were as steady as nailheads and as bright as if the nailheads had been polished.

"Gosh a'mighty," said Red from over the tops of his guns. "Don't you understand sign language? Get your hands up!"

The gambler flipped up his palms but scarcely raised his elbows off the table.

In the midst of the startled hum and broken babble, Hamel half arose from his chair, face angrily darkened, and shouted, "Here! What do you mean—"

"Feller, keep the bottom of your pants on that chair," Red told him.

"B-but—" Hamel shouted with stuttering explosiveness.

"Or the carpenter'll be making you a suit of clothes to wear in hell," Red added cheerfully.

Hamel settled back in staring amazement, as if not quite understanding, as if wondering, too, if this lanky stranger to Tajola wholly understood just what he was doing.

Apparently he did, for Red added, "And you other hombres, if any of you love this tinhorn well enough to cut in on my play, you're welcome."

The young fellow, who also had red hair, twisted about with startled interest, gazing up over his shoulder.

"My gosh. Brothers," said someone, noticing that the two redheads were about of an age.

"Who the hell are you?" Hamel shouted.

Red started to answer, but the young gambler who had dealt was sitting to the right of the young fellow who had just lost his pile; and, with shrinking twist of body, he crouched low and to one side with his hand out of sight under the breast of his coat. Red, without any warning at all, suddenly leaned forward and with downward swing of the long barrel in his right hand cracked Wolf Face's head.

16

"A feller that can't sneak the draw no better'n, that ought not to try," said Red critically.

As the unconscious man slumped out of his chair, the men standing there saw a short nickel-plated gun lying beside him. A bystander picked it up and, the better to appear neutral, held it by the muzzle.

"Jack! You and Frank!" Hamel shouted toward the cowmen sitting in the game. "Are you going to let this—"

"Is your socks clean?" Red asked, eyeing Hamel. "'Cause if you don't keep that foodtrap locked, I'll plug her up with your own big toe!" Bystanders snickered. Hamel, a big man in the town, who bossed folks about and thought well of himself, had a look of painful amazement. "Some silence outa you, and a lot of it, will be most pleasing," Red added.

There was an unhurried, slightly good-natured way about Red that did not make Hamel or the gambler feel more comfortable. They knew that he wasn't drunk and he wasn't scared.

The two cowmen, Jack Harris and Frank Sterns, gazed at him with squint-eyed suspicion. They seemed right on edge to interfere yet hesitated, because they, and the other folk who stood about the table, sensed that Red was calling a showdown on the gambler; and if he could make it good, all right. Harris and Sterns had lost enough to feel some pleasure in seeing the gambler in a tight hole.

17

The gambler sat pale and steady, with eyes unwinking as a snake's. His arms were crooked at the elbows with the palms out and lifted, but his elbows almost touched the table. He asked in a husky, anxious sort of tone, "Gentlemen, gentlemen, you going to stand for this?"

Some of the bystanders cleared their throats, but no one spoke. Only those directly behind the menaced gambler had moved, shifting with hasty clack of high-heeled boots to right and left.

"Gambler, what's your name?" Red asked in the unhurried voice of a man who had been through this sort of thing time and again and knew there was no need for haste.

"I'm Perley Price and a square gambler!"

"I'm sure glad to hear that," said Red commendingly. "Now how about histing your hands up—away up—plumb straight up as high as you can get 'em?"

The gambler's lips tightened and a moment's stare of hopelessness crossed his eyes, but he said nothing. Hamel's fat face grew red, then paled to the look of an overcooked beet.

"Speak up, Perley Price," said Red encouragingly. "Folks is listening."

Price moved his lips nervously. The shadow of fear lay on his tense white face. They were big guns that he looked into, and the hands that held them were sinewy and steady. The face that looked down over them had the twisted smile and blue snap of eye that signified a man who was dangerous even if amused.

Price seemed to heave at his arms but did not lift them. "I—I've got rheumatism and can't—can't—"

"Yeah?"

"Once I was shot in the shoulder, the left shoulder. It's stiff," said Perley Price hastily.

Red laughed at him. "Poke them arms up, feller—or pay back all your winnings."

Silence followed. Men peered inquiringly at Red, glanced with hasty questioning from one to another, eyed the gambler with suspicions, vague but highly unfavorable. They were mystified, yet understood clearly enough that the gambler was somehow caught. Price looked a little as if he were being choked. Twice he started to lift his arms but he never raised them far and at last settled his elbows on the table as if, indeed, some kind of pain made him wince.

Men watched staringly. Hamel's big heavy face grew almost chalky as he stuttered, wanting onlookers to cut in and make Red back out.

"F-fellers, stop this damn fool," he demanded.

"Huh," said a big, bearded old-timer who looked more like a miner than a cowman, speaking clear and loud. "You're wearing a gun, Hamel. Stop him yourself. Be inter-resting to see."

Men waited breathlessly, eyeing the gambler who played his part, like a man half frozen, with much cold nerve; but he was caught and daringly hesitated, hoping somebody might help him out. But nobody stirred. Most men thought that Red, though a stranger in town, had cut the gambler's trail before and so had something on him, for Red was so confident and seemed to know what he was about.

Then there was the spurred jingle of shuffling feet coming over the saloon floor at a dog trot, and a moment later a slow voice in mournful reproach declared, "Well, I'll be damned if he ain't started something already."

Buck Waxman's tall, rangy body straightened up behind the encircling group and, peering over, he added in weary drone of voice, "Price, you'd better do what the kid tells you, 'cause if you don't, you'll have a mighty skimpy funeral, with most mourners cheerful."

"Well," said Price slowly, with good self-control, though he showed plenty of strain, "if anybody thinks I don't play square, I'm ready to— to—to—" it gave him a lot of pain to say it, but he squeezed out the words—"to pay back."

"Not much you don't!" said the young fellow who had lost his money. "When I play poker, I pay."

"You ain't been playing poker, son," Red snapped. "You been—"

"I said I'd pay," Price interrupted hastily in a high-pitched voice.

He began counting chips and money and putting them into sacks. He also took chips from the pile of his unconscious partner and pushing them toward Hamel, who was banking the game, said, "Pay him!"

"Not me," said the young fellow with a gesture of refusal. "When I lose, I lose!"

"Coax him, Hamel," Red suggested.

Bystanders, now pretty clearly understanding that Red somehow knew that the gambler had cheated, clucked, "Take it, kid." "It's yours, son." "Be a bigger fool not to take it than you was to lose it." "I wish I'd had me a red-headed friend like him standing behind me in some of the poker games I been in."

Hamel, seeing how sentiment ran, counted over the money and with a bad grace pushed it to the young man, saying, "She's yours, since Price wants to give it back. That shows it's been a square game, don't it?"

"Yeah," said Jack Harris, "in which case I'm next in line to be persuaded it's been square."

"Me, too," said Frank Sterns with enthusiasm.

"But see here, boys," Hamel protested severely, "you ain't going to be pikers and squeal? Besides—" Hamel frowned, leaving much unsaid.

"'Besides' be damned!" said Harris, glaring defiantly at Hamel. "I don't know what it's all about, but—" he whipped up a gun and leveled it straight at Price—"me and Frank here have dropped over a thousand dollars. And if anybody's going to be paid, we want in on it. What do you say, gambler?"

"My game's on the square. Ask Hamel. He's known me a long time. But I'll pay."

"If folks don't like losing, you pay 'em back. That's sure being on the square," said the bearded old-timer.

The young poker player, seeing that other losers in the game were collecting, at last clearly enough understood that something had been wrong and that he was as much entitled to have his money back as if the gambler had been a pickpocket. He stacked a pile of twenties, picked them up and twisting about in his chair, turned with hand uplifted to offer Red a reward. But Red Clark had gone.

"Who was he?" the young man asked.

"Who, eh? Yes, who was that fool kid?"

"Who knows? I never seen him before."

"Waxman knowed him."

"Waxman? Hey, Waxman!"

"Hell, old Waxman's gone, too."

"Cool hombre."

"Yeah, for a kid."

"Kid, hell! His guns were man-sized."

"Sneaked off," said Hamel, rising up and looking about as if hopeful of finding Red near.

"I hope he don't run out of town," said Mr. Perley Price who had stooped solicitously over the unconscious Wolf Face, whom Red had whammed over the head with the gun barrel. "Trying to make it appear my game ain't straight."

"Feller," said the old-timer, "I wouldn't get all overhet from hurrying to find that young un. No, I wouldn't. You get all in a sweat, you might catch cold sudden. Yeah!"

CHAPTER 3.

The Puncher With Three Names

Red was in his room at the hotel. He sat in the only chair. His boots were off and his guns hung on the bedpost. With his back to the lamp he was trying, without much interest, to read an old newspaper, now and then eyeing the partition through which came the sizzle, pop, and splutter of a noisy sleeper.

"Yessir," Red mused, "if he ever gets married and his wife shoots him, me, I'm going to testify she done right. Sounds like he was sawing through an empty rain barrel."

Footsteps came along the hall, stopped; then there was a tapping on the door.

"I'm not doing it," Red called. "It's coming from the next room. But he won't wake up. I've tried."

"It's me. Can I see you?"

"Lots of folks call themselves 'me.' Which one are you?" Red asked, rising.

"The boy who was playing poker and—"

"Oh, you, hunh?" said Red, opening the door.

"I've come to warn you," the young fellow exclaimed nervously.

"Now ain't that nice. Come in and set. You think them tinhorns are going to lay for me, unh?"

Red, closing the door and pointing toward the chair, grinned at him.

"How do you know that?" asked the boy.

"Son, I know the breed. Personally I never associate with gamblers, 'less they've got a rope 'round their neck. I play some poker, but always there must be some calluses on the hands of the fellows I play with."

"I was in a back room. Wanted to be alone and think. In the dark. I heard the gamblers talking. They said—"

Red nodded. "I reckon. They're going to lay for me, unh?"

"Why, yes, but how did you guess?"

"Shucks, son! Now and then I stomp on folks's tails. Tinhorns are snakes that have learned to walk on two legs. Step on their tails, and they try to bite when you aren't looking. A good, honest old rattler don't give a damn whether you're looking or not. It's why I like rattlers better'n some folks. What's your name, son?"

"Oh, well, call me Smith and let it go at that."

24

"Nope. I won't. It's a good name, but supposing in a crowd I was suddenly to sing out, 'Hey, Smithy!' Now, set down."

The young man sat down on the only chair. Red dropped onto the bed, drew out tobacco and papers and offered them.

"Thanks." As the young fellow rolled a cigarette, he glanced up, looking Red over in an admiring way, and said, "I wish you'd tell me something. It puzzled me. Puzzled other people, too. They were all talking about it. You must have known that gambler was cheating and—"

"And why didn't I plug him? Well, sir, 'tain't what some folks call etiquette for a bystander to shoot card sharks. Those who are setting in his game have what you call first rights. But I'll make a confession, son—" Red was not much older than this boy he called "son"—"I didn't know he was cheatin'."

"You didn't?"

"Nope. I've known some honest gamblers, but mostly they were broke half the time. And I've seen some dead gamblers that wasn't honest. I'm not onto all the tricks a gambler can play, any more than I can outguess the devil. But Mr. Perley Price held his cards like he wore a contraption that is called a holdout. Now, I'm curious. It's a weakness with me, being curious. So I sort of experimented. If he'd raised his arms clear up, his cuffs would've dropped. Everybody would have seen whether or not he was wearing one."

"What if he had lifted his arms and there hadn't been a holdout?"

"I'd have had to do a hell of a lot of apologizing—maybe. I'm an awful poor hand to apologize. Makes me feel bad. I'd have been in a pickle, sure. But I was betting with myself that he wouldn't raise his arms. I'm lucky when I don't show no sense. It's got to be a habit with me—being lucky."

"But if he had raised his arms, sudden-like, and there'd been a holdout," the young fellow asked, "would you have shot him?"

Red grinned. "Hunh. I reckon not. If he'd shown a holdout, my guns would've been as superfluous as an old sweetheart at a fellow's wedding. Those two wicked-eyed hombres, Harris and Sterns, would've made him look like a lobsided doughnut. You see—"

Red stopped, listening. The rumble of snores in the next room had taken on a shriller pitch. Red knocked on the partition. The snores stopped momentarily. "Some folks are disagreeable even in their sleep."

"I feel I owe you something for what you did," said the young man and put a hand down deep into his pocket.

Red shook his head. "How'd a kid your size and age ever get hold of that much money?" he asked.

"I don't know."

"Yeah?" Red asked distrustfully.

"Yes. My mother died when I was a boy in school back East, four or five years ago. I didn't like it there, so I came back to the ranch of the old man up in Colorado where she had been living—he had been a friend to my grandfather, or something. He was one of those old-timers who won't talk much. Anyhow, I was twenty-one not long ago, and one day this old man took me into town to the bank and said I had five thousand dollars coming. Said my mother had left it for me. I didn't know what to do with it. Then this old-timer died and the ranch was sold. One day, about a month ago, I was in town, and a fellow who works in the post office told me there was a letter for me. I went in and got it. Here it is—"

He drew out an envelope and offered it to Red. Red leaned forward and eyed the envelope without touching it. The address was to Mr. Jerry Douglas, Turdoz, Colorado.

"You him?" Red asked.

"Yes. Read the letter. Then you'll understand why I'm so puzzled."

"Umh," said Red and gingerly fingered the letter. It was written in pencil, laboriously, as if by one not used to writing. It said:

"Dear sir, I know all about you and how you are now twenty-one years old. Maybe I'm getting myself in a hell of a lot of

27

trouble in telling you to come down here to Tajola, but come anyhow, son. Whatever you do, don't let nobody know your name is Jerome Douglas. I knew your mother well and I know all about your dad, which you don't. When you come to Tajola you stick around town and sort of give out that your name is Frank Peters and I'll look you up and try to help you. I know all about everything and I'm doing it more for another fellow than for you. He's alright but an awful fool, the same as most folks, and me too, maybe. You come, son. You'll find me a friend. Yours truly."

There was no signature.

"Hmm," said Red. "Curious."

"I came to town yesterday. But somehow I was a little afraid to use the name of Peters, like this letter says to, before I had looked around. Of course, I didn't use my own name. I just called myself Smith. I don't know what to make of it. I feel queer and uneasy about it."

Red grunted noncommittally and began rereading the letter.

"I had all that money in a satchel," young Douglas went on, "and I got to playing poker. There was nothing much else to do. Tonight I got deep into the game and couldn't quit and somehow didn't care. A while ago, when I overheard

28

the gamblers talking, I felt I just had to find you and warn you, so I came over here to the hotel and asked if—"

Red had folded the letter and was putting it back into the envelope when he heard shuffling steps along the hall and a knock on his door.

"Yeah? What you want?" he asked, standing up, eyeing the door, and unconsciously slipping the letter into the breast pocket of his shirt.

"Old Buck Waxman has been bad hurt and is asking for you, mister," a voice called through the closed door. "Will you come?"

"You're damn tooting!" said Red and with a backhanded sweep of his right hand he whisked a gun from its holster at the foot of the bed, at the same time jerking open the door.

A small, old, bowlegged man in dirty blue overalls and with bleary eyes stood there. He flung both hands up rigidly, made a sound as if poked in the belly, and kept his mouth wide open.

"'Smatter, Shorty?" Red asked, lowering the gun. "You act like you'd seen a ghost. Come in and set down."

The frowzy old loafer stammered and shifted his feet, hesitating, wanting to go away, but not daring. "I just come with word like I was told," he whined.

"Well, you just come along in here like you've been told, too."

Shorty came in. He stopped with sudden pop of

eye at the Douglas boy and blinked. Two redheads of about an age in the same little room almost made the old loafer think he was seeing double.

"Sit down," said Red, reaching for his boots.

Shorty sat gingerly on the edge of the bed. Red, standing on one foot, began to slip on a boot, and asked, "Who sent you, Shorty?"

"Wh-why a feller. Old Waxman, he's been—"

Red snorted impatiently. "Listen, feller. If an angel came and told me, I'd know 'twasn't so. Listen. You hear that sound like a barrel full of tin cans rolling downhill? That's old Buck snoring. I've had to crawl out and leave him all the blankets too many times not to know. Besides, he didn't ride out of town like folks thought tonight there at the corral. He changed his mind and put his horse in the stable behind the hotel, then came up and talked with me a while. After which he went to bed. So for your information and so you won't have any doubts, I'm telling you you're a liar. And a danged poor one. It's awful wrong, Shorty, to tell lies. Who's laying for me?"

Red had got into his boots and was buckling on his guns.

"Wh-why—er—I—I—d-don't know nothing and—" Shorty stopped, not liking the way Red was eyeing him. "I come like I was told."

"Who told you?"

"A—er—f-feller."

"Name?"

"I n-never seen 'im be-before."

"And most likely won't ever see him again," said Red, reaching for a gun.

"Ow—it was Hamel," Shorty blurted, shrinking, with his eyes on the gun and with about the same expression on his face as if he had awakened in bed and found his nose near a rattlesnake. "But he'll kill me if he knows I told you."

"What you grumbling about? You need killing, don't you? Coming over here to coax a nice boy like me into a trap. Who's laying for me and where?"

"I don't know. Honest, mister. Hamel said for me to come and tell you Waxman had been hurt and was laying down to the Stage Company barn, asking for you. So I come and—I wouldn't've come if—if—I'd thought Hamel meant to do you dirt."

"Yeah, you're so kind-hearted it shows in your face, like a boil on a skinny nose. So they want me to come waltzing into the Stage Company barn, hunh? Son—" this to young Douglas—"I hate to be unsociable but I'm going out to get some fresh air."

"But you're not, surely, going down there?" exploded Douglas, rising. "Let me—I'll go with you and—Why, they mean to kill you!"

"Go off and leave Shorty, here all by his lonesome? No, we can't do that. You keep him company. And if I don't come back, Buck Waxman'll wear his ears for a watch charm."

"I'll wear 'em myself," said young Douglas,

31

frowning at Shorty, who twisted a foot about an ankle, hunched his shoulders, and peered up anxiously with watery, booze-reddened eyes. "You damned dirty . . ." Douglas in nervous anger cursed him at length. "Just as much a murderer as if you'd shot him in the back yourself."

Shorty's slack mouth hung open like a flytrap.

Red listened critically and interrupted commendingly with, "I reckon being to school back East does sort of help a fellow cuss some. I've always heard that education was a good thing to have. You sure do speak fluent. Shorty's eyes are just a-popping out with the joys of learning. He feels like he'd bumped his nose on a hornet's nest, don't you, Shorty? Shorty ain't no killer, are you, Shorty? You've kicked a crippled dog now and then, maybe, ain't you? He's so peaceable he don't even carry a gun. Or is it 'cause a gun'd sort of get in your way while you were emptying spittoons and sweeping out Hamel's saloon? Right now Shorty is most prayerful that I'll come back, sound and whole—or without no holes—ain't you, Shorty? Yeah, of course you are. The kid, here, needs some ears a-dangling on his watch chain to dress him up, and you've got handsome ears, Shorty. 'By, kid."

Red opened the door, stepped through, and pulled it to. The clank of his spurs rattled as he went along the hall at the stride of a man hurrying.

"Wh-who is he?" Shorty asked a little breathlessly as he wiped his forehead with a dirty palm and blinked at the closed door.

"I don't know who he is," said Douglas. "But he's the best friend I've got. And if he gets hurt, I'll kill you, you dirty . . ." Douglas again cursed him angrily, nervously, with feeling.

CHAPTER 4.

The Barkeep Who Said Nothing

Red went down the stairs and turned into the hotel barroom. The barkeep was half asleep with a cigarette smoldering in his fingers. No one else was there.

The bartender straightened up in the chair where he was idling and said, "Old Crawley came a while ago looking for you."

"Who's he?"

"He ain't much of nobody. A kind of sweeper-out down to the Stage Barn, and—"

"A sawed-off runt what looks scairt of water? Yeah, he found me. Brought me word from a feller. Tell me, who owns the Stage Company?"

"Huh? Say, who owns most near everything in Tajola? Hamel does."

"I was just curious. Left my horse down there this afternoon when I rode in. Mind telling me the time? I had a nice watch once, but a slab-sided

33

piece of lightning that was covered with horse hair up and flung me kiting. I hit the ground so hard that watch wouldn't keep time any more."

"She's twenty of twelve," the bartender said, pulling out a watch as big as a biscuit. "I shut up at twelve when business is like now. Say—" the bartender's eyes glowed with new interest—"was it you that horned in on that poker game over to the Cross Bar tonight?"

"I was among them present."

"You're most likely to be among the missing, too, if you don't take care," said the bartender with a confidential drop to his tone, looking Red over from hat to boots.

"You think maybe I ought to hit leather and kick up some dust?"

"I would," said the bartender with confessional frankness. "Folks have a way of dying of lead poisoning—mysterious—down in this country." The barkeep nodded slowly. "Savvy?"

"No," said Red. "I don't savvy why grown men that ain't cripples put up with it."

The bartender, who wasn't a young man, looked at him carefully, glanced toward the door, then ran his eyes all about as if to make sure that no listeners had slipped in. Then he went behind the bar and without a word put out two glasses and pushed the bottle toward Red. Red poured a short drink. The bartender filled his own glass, grunted, "Here's how," and tossed the liquor at his mouth.

Then with elbows on the bar he leaned forward, eyed Red, and spoke.

"Listen, son," he said, "I ain't one of them strong, silent men who keeps their mouths shut 'cause they don't like to talk. I do it 'cause I don't want to get shot. I've worked in places where bullets hummed like hornets, and I've squatted down on the floor, mighty neutral, and held my breath. Yeah, like before you're married you do when waiting to see if the girl is going to say she'll marry you. Or like after you're married you do when you're waiting to see if the old lady is going to believe that that there blond hair was put on your shoulder by a feller who was playing a joke. You ever been married?"

"So far, my bad luck hasn't taken that form."

"Women are queer folks, 'specially after they get to be your wives." The bartender gazed reflectively at the ceiling, then sighed. "I come down to Tajola a short while ago and took this here job because my home life wasn't happy. Have another drink?"

Red took another short one. The bartender filled his own glass.

"I ain't been here long and I'm quitting. In a way of speaking, you and me are both strangers to these parts. Like I was saying, I don't mind a little commotionate shindig now and then. It's plumb customary in a barroom. I know some folks say it ain't mannerly for a barkeep to dodge, sort of intimates that the boys exercising their trigger fingers ain't trustworthy. I don't like to insult no customers, but I got hesitations about being polite enough to get buried. But—"

The talkative bartender again looked about carefully, then filled his glass once more.

"I been here three weeks," he said. "There ain't been what you'd call a shooting scrape in all that time, but—" his voice dropped to a husky, uneasy whisper—"but three men have been killed, mysterious. Shot down on the street in the dark or killed out near the edge of town. I hear tell that out on the range men have been dying mysterious like that off and on for a year."

"Hmmm," said Red, noncommittal but encouraging. Old Buck Waxman had hinted at something of the kind, but old Buck was about as uninformative as a signpost that has blown down. Red listened well, seemed interested but a little skeptical. It was quiet and lonely in the saloon, suitable for indiscreet gossip, and the bartender was just aching to talk freely.

He said, "You're a stranger and leaving town, ain't you?"

"I'm a stranger," Red agreed, "and I ain't got no hankering for sojourning permanent in Tajola. And I wouldn't want to put strangers to the trouble of burying me. I'm thoughtful that way. So I figure that right soon I'll slip out the back way and go down to the Stage barn. That's where my horse is."

"That's right," said the bartender, approving.

"Strangers have a way of getting killed in Tajola. 'Specially if they're nosy and meddlesome. One of them fellers that got killed recent—it was a mistake. He was just a train robber, sort of vacationing, but he went about watchful and listening, so folks misunderstood his motives. The other two had been hired to nose about. But they ran up against a cold deck. Must have been that somebody was onto 'em, 'cause they'd just come to town, had some supper, took a couple of drinks right here at this bar, and went for a little walk. 'Bout ten minutes later they was dead, shot in the back, and the next morning they was took across the arroyo and buried—careful. Coyotes're bad hereabouts. One thing you've got to say for Tajola. Folks get a deep grave. Some writing was found in their pockets, which told as how they was detectives. Poor ones, I'd say. A detective that gets detected is as out of luck as a woman that shows her age."

"Hamel kill 'em?" Red asked bluntly.

The bartender gave a little start, glanced hastily about the barroom, then had another glass of whisky. "My good gosh," he said in a low voice, "you are some pointed in your remarks."

"Shucks, I hear tell that Hamel even owns the woodpile from which coffins is made. Every business man likes to do what he can to make trade lively."

The bartender shied off a little and eyed Red in unfriendly meditation.

"I can't recollect that I mentioned names a-tall," he said and looked at his watch. "She's twelve o'clock. My hours of pretending to labor is all done." He untied his apron and turned toward a peg, then glanced over his shoulder and shook his head. "You ain't going to make a handsome corpse," he observed.

"You're right. I'm too skinny. Makes me hard to hit and easy missed, too. So I ain't going to be a corpse of any kind. But you've got no call to shy at Hamel's name like you'd seen a ghost. I hit town today innocent as a lamb that straggles into a butcher shop, sort of friendly and curious. Then I horned in on the game of some blackleg tinhorns. They were Hamel's friends. He knows they're crooked as a cross-eyed dog's hind leg. All right. You being a good feller, and fatherly, you tell me to up-tail and skeedaddle. Now, when I follow your advice and run, who the hell am I running from if I'm not running from Hamel?"

The bartender gazed with blank-eyed confusion before Red's logic and murmured, "I ought to've kept my mouth shut."

"No, sir. You ought to open her wide and give me some of your hidden thoughts. I'm curious. I won't squeal. Tell me, why does a man like Hamel, who owns a cow outfit and must have plenty of money, throw in with tinhorns? What's wrong with this country anyhow? Men getting killed. Rustling going on. Hell a-popping like eggs in hot ashes, and everybody saying, 'Shh-hh-h! We mustn't talk about it.' Oh, it ain't just you. I got a friend who's an old-timer and so danged tough that cactuses draw in their stickers and curl up when he comes close. A rattler bit him once and the poor snake throwed a fit like D.T.s and rolled over, belly up, and died. Well, sir, we talked some tonight up in my room, and he hinted and hedged and wrapped himself up in silence like a peevish Injun when I asked questions. He isn't scared of anything on two legs or four—if they don't wear skirts. He likes me fine and would trust me with his last half pint of water in hell or whisky in camp. But he won't answer questions any more'n a deef mute that's died of lockjaw. Here—" Red shoved the bottle at the bartender and pulled out a gold coin—"have one on me."

The bartender pushed back the money but filled his glass and fingering it, spoke.

"Listen. Folks hereabouts don't talk much 'cause they don't know what's what or who's who. Things are mysterious. I'm sort of a stranger, too, down in these parts, but ears are to listen with. You say you're leaving town, which is sensible. Do you by happenchance know about old Monroe of the Zee Zee?"

"I've heard the name."

"Well, him and Hamel are friends." The bartender stopped, nodded significantly, and appeared to feel that he had told everything.

"Yeah? Well, go on."

"You don't appear to understand."

"You guessed it."

"Hmmm," said the bartender. Then, with a meditative eye on Red he added, "I reckon you don't know much about old Jerry Monroe."

"I've heard tell he's a bad one to monkey with." The numerous whiskies had warmed the bartender's tongue, somewhat loosened his discretion.

"Son, he is a devil in pants. Sour, silent, and hard. He don't give a damn for nothing or nobody, including himself. Only Hamel. That's why Hamel does as he damn pleases. Old Jerry Monroe'll back him up, and behind Monroe ride hellbenders right off the headwaters of Bitter Creek. Hamel himself is nothing but a barkeep who somehow made friends with Monroe twenty years ago. You asked why he throwed in with tinhorn gamblers. I'll tell you."

The bartender lowered his voice. "Monroe's Zee Zee punchers make the Cross Bar Saloon their hangout. They get trimmed at poker. Miners come in. Tinhorns rob 'em. Hamel'd cheat his mother out of the filling of her last tooth. He's bad, plumb bad. He appoints the judge and elects the sheriff. He's worked himself up, with Monroe's backing, till he's a pretty big cowman, but his instincts keep him still a low-breed saloon keeper. Folks are afraid of Monroe."

"These range killings? Who does 'em?" Red asked.

40

"Well, I hear talk and I'm telling you. Ain't I telling you?"

"Plenty."

"All right. Listen. Folks don't know who's doing 'em. They do say that Jerry Monroe don't fight in the dark or shoot in the back. Besides, some of his men have been killed, too. Folks say Monroe suspicions Oliver Morgan of the Bar O Bar, who holds the range north of Rasalis Divide. You know Oliver Morgan?"

"Heard the name."

"He's a big cowman. Not like Monroe. Married. Got a family. Pretty wife. Nice girls. Monroe hates women worse'n a drunk hates pink elephants. Can't stand 'em. That's what's the matter with him. His wife ran off with a puncher, or he drove her off, or something. Before that he was a human being. Since then he's been a terror. Everybody hates him. Always fighting with his neighbors. Ain't got a friend living—'cept Hamel. That's why I been telling you you better get to hell out of Tajola, son. Pronto! Savvy?"

"I'll go right down to where my horse is," said Red, starting toward the door.

"Remember," the bartender called, "I ain't said nothing. Don't you repeat what I've told you. If you do, I'll call you a liar."

"I'll be one if I ever peep," said Red and pushed through the back door of the saloon.

Schmaling Mem. Pub. Library
501 Tenth Avenue
Fulton, IL 61252

CHAPTER 5.

Red Comes A-shooting

The hotel sat alone on a corner, facing the street, which was unlighted, except for splotches of lamplight that fell through the open doorways of two or three saloons far up the street where a few men were still loitering at bars or gambling.

It was a moonless night, with stars flickering like distant windblown torches. Shadows were heavy, with a tinge of the desert's purplish blackness in them, and silence like a great presence holding its breath was over the town.

As Red stepped out of the rear door into the quiet night the tinkle of his spurs sounded loud. "Like I was wearing jinglebobs," he said to himself. He paused, unbuckled them, and rammed them into his hip pockets. It was not comfortable. Pockets were not shaped to carry spurs. "Now I'm feeling what a horse has to put up with all the time. I'd buck, too, if somebody was setting on my back, jabbing them things in my ribs." Half unconsciously, from habit, he loosened his guns in their holsters, wanting to be certain that they would come slick and free when he reached for them.

The Stage Company had its barn, corral, and

pasture out toward the edge of town. Tajola was a small town.

He was going the back way just to make sure that the clever hombres who had sent Shorty with the false message would not have a chance at him in case they had decided not to wait at the corral but to ambush him on the way.

Red talked silently to himself as he went along. "I was a smart baby to pick out for a dad a fellow who was an old Injun fighter. It's no disgrace to be careful, as the widow woman said when she had 'em put a big rock on her husband's grave. I wasn't in any great shakes of a hurry, 'cause I figured on showing up over here just about the time those fellows got to thinking maybe me and Shorty wasn't coming. When surprise parties are planned, it's always well to do your part. Makes 'em more entertaining. Maybe I will light out tomorrow, but tonight—why, my own shadow would be ashamed to follow me if I backed off from this little celebration that has been arranged for me, special."

Red's hand half unconsciously fumbled at the breast pocket of his shirt where he kept tobacco and papers. He felt something unfamiliar.

"Gosh. I carried off that Douglas kid's letter. Shorty coming like he did made me forgetful. Maybe I hadn't better smoke yet a while. Maybe there'll be plenty of smoke right soon. That barkeep sort of took the hobbles off his tongue, didn't he?"

43

Crouching low and using as well as he could the scant shadows of yucca, cactus, and whatever else cast its skeleton outline in the starlight, Red worked around back of the stake corral. Then, from a distance, he heard a shot. He hung motionless, poised and listening.

"Hmm. That was uptown. Just one shot. If my ears are doing their duty, that wasn't a sixgun. Maybe somebody was inviting old Buck to stop snoring. Buck's funny. He makes an awful racket when he sleeps. You can yell and cuss and kick and beat a dishpan, and he won't hear you. But just you put a foot down cautious, snap a twig, or cock a gun, and he's setting up, waiting."

Red came up to the high stake corral but could not climb over without a lot of scrambling that would have silhouetted him against the light of the sky. "In which case it might be a lobsided surprise party, with me on the fence like a one-legged chicken. When I point my hind end toward trouble, I like to be horseback, not hanging over a fence."

He crawled under the barbed wire into the pasture where there were the lumpy shadows of horses that dozed standing and lying down. Some of the horses stirred, rose, shook themselves, eyed him with questioning, forward flip of ears, and moved away slowly.

Red walked along the corral to where a row of crossbars served as a gate. He peered through into the corral and saw two or three wagons and a stage with a wheel off. He crept through, drew near the barn, and paused to listen. The dusty ground was littered with straw, making a soft cushion for his tiptoes.

The barn faced the street, with a wide high runway clear through to the street. Men who were tall in the saddle could ride through on the lope without stooping. Red, keeping well in the shadows, edged nearer and nearer. He grinned as he heard the faint drone of a voice. The words were indistinct, but the tone was sharp with irritation.

"Maybe he won't be so disappointed as he thinks he is," said Red to himself.

There was, of course, always somebody on duty at the barn; but barn bosses were usually asleep at night—and half asleep in the daytime, too. Usually they didn't have visitors after midnight.

When Red got to where he could peer into the wide high runway, he saw that two lanterns were hung on pegs. They were smoky yellow, dusty lanterns that cut the shadows into queer heavy blocks.

"Thoughtful gazebos. Yeah. They thought I'd come ramping in, all out of breath in a hurry, and have them lights in my eyes."

A horse shifted its feet and rattled its halter in a stall. This horse was kept up so that the barn boss could drive in the horses from the pasture. Red edged along noiselessly, crouching and on tiptoes.

He made out the shadow of a man between him and the light. The man's back was to him and he sat hunched over on a bucket.

" 'Tain't no use to wait any longer. He ain't coming."

"We'd better wait." This voice came from near the doorway. Then Red saw dimly a figure leaning against the doorway, keeping a watch up the street.

"I don't like it," said a third voice.

"My gosh!" Red thought. "This here reception committee is plumb numerous, though one of 'em may be the barn roustabout, who thinks he ain't going to take part."

"I don't think he's coming," said the man on the bucket. "We been waiting a hell of a long time."

"He ain't coming," said the unseen third man who was squatting in the shadows. "I think you'd be sort of glad, Jack. He saved you some money in that poker game."

"Orders is orders, ain't they? Hamel's got us where the wool's short, ain't he? Besides, he swore up and down those gamblers was square. I don't know. But I do know which side my bread's buttered on."

"Why don't he let Price and Timkins do their own shooting?"

"Why, he says this redhead is another detective. We gotta get rid of him. That's all."

"He ain't coming," said the unseen man again

with a kind of stubborn intonation. "I bet he ain't. Maybe he's too smart."

"Well, somebody's coming," the man at the door announced. "And running. Get ready, Jack."

The man on the bucket jumped up, drew a gun, and sidled into the shadows. "You lay there still, Bob," he said, "like you was hurt. He's expecting to find Waxman bad hurt."

When the man on the bucket moved, Red had a look at his face in the lantern light. He was one of the cowmen who had been in the poker game.

For a time all was silence, except for the stir of the horse's halter rope as he tossed his head and shifted his feet. Then the man who was cautiously keeping watch at the door said, "Hell, 'tain't him a-tall. It's Tom Brown. Hey, Tom, what's the matter?"

"We got 'im, boys!" a voice called exultantly, and a man appeared in the doorway. A lanky man with a long, twisted nose and a twisted mouth, who had come hurrying with news and now strutted a bit as he came into the barn with the men gathering close about him.

"Yeah, we got 'im, sure. Y'see, me and Frank was watching across the street to see him and old Crawley come out and head down this way. He didn't come. No, sir. He musta smelt a mouse or somethin'. Well, me and Frank got tired of waiting. We knew something was wrong. So I started scouting around. Went around to the side of the hotel where I saw a light. I looked up, and there, by God, through the window I could see him plain. I called Frank, and we both looked. So help me, fellers, we could make out that he had old Crawley there in his room. So Frank, he runs down to the saloon, gets Hamel's .38-40, and hustles back. We waits and waits and when he moved up close to the window, Frank let him have it. Didn't you hear the shot?"

"Sure. You mean he suspicioned old Crawley? But hell, Tom, Crawley himself didn't know it was a put-up job."

"I don't know nothing about that. Frank and me ducked away over to the saloon, put back the rifle, and had some drinks quiet-like. Then Hamel said for me to jog trot down here and tell you boys to come along in. Another smart aleck is going to be carted over to the graveyard in the morning."

"And he don't go alone, you—" Red Clark came out of the shadows as if thrown. The blackest oaths he knew rippled, vivid as gun flame, on his lips. Thinking to kill him, they had shot the other red-headed boy from the dark, in the back. Red wasn't cautious when he was angered. He knew these men for dirty killers and he was an honest, hard-working boy with the blood of honest, hard-fighting frontiersmen forefathers pouring courage into his heart.

The startled men spun about, gasping, yelping in

48

surprise, jerking at guns, swearing through wide-open mouths as if at a ghost, for at the first flickering glimpse they had recognized him. The lash of gunfire cut the shadows. The mingling roar of .45s echoed through the barn, shook the rafters, and smoke went up in puff on puff, dimming the yellow glow of the lanterns.

They had fired with hasty twitch of hands to thigh; and Red, with guns out in hip-low aim, laced their group with lead. They were bad men, the lot of them; but Red was the son of an old sheriff who had done much to teach desperadoes that honest men could be as reckless and more dangerous than outlaws themselves. There was a wild flurry of shooting, with men leaping for shelter and falling dead as if tripped hellward, and smoking guns were flung on the ground. Tom Brown crumpled with the dead center of his forehead splattered by a little black hole, gone to the devil marked purposefully with Red's vengeance. Harris dropped trickily, belly down, and fired twice, then rolled over in a spasmodic writhing, whipping legs and arms about and clawing at the thick dust. Bob, the barn boss, frantically shot a time or two, then with zigzag leaps made for the door. He threw snap shots backward as he glanced over his shoulder. Then he pitched headlong through the doorway, arms and legs outspread, face down in the dust.

The other man, known as Buster, jumped behind

a post and with an arm out on each side shot rapidly but blindly, hoping for luck.

Red, taught from early boyhood to keep count of his shots, stopped shooting. He simply stood and waited, as if frozen, in a low half crouch with one gun leveled. Buster, thinking one of his own bullets had struck, peered around the post and ducked too late. The guns fell from his hands and, grasping the post, hugging it, he slid down and lay still.

Red stood still, breathing deeply, with empty guns down-tilted, and blinked through the smoky silence. Scarcely a half minute had passed from the time he had jumped into the fight, and here he stood alone. His hat was gone, whether shot away or shaken off he did not know. There was a warm trickle of something sticky down his leg but no pain, and the leg wasn't weak. Red blinked again through the smoky haze and took a step backward. He peered as if seeing things that couldn't be, wiped at his eyes with a forearm, and leaned forward.

Looming in the barn doorway was a horse and rider, and the horse was coming at the slowest of walks with ears flickering in out-tilted inquiry. A big, long-legged black horse and in the saddle a tall man. The horse, with careful placing of feet, stepped over the body of the dead barn boss and came on. The tall rider sat motionless with hands on the horn and riding close, right into the lantern light, stopped and peered down.

His face was dark as old cowhide and bony, masklike and marked with evilness, but there wasn't a weak spot in it; and the eyes had a frowning stare, straight as a knife blade and as sharp. Red had a queer sensation, as if face to face with something that wasn't quite human, as with a kind of groping vagueness he realized that this horseman must have been in the road out there, right in line with stray bullets, watching. Now he rode right into the lingering smoke of the fight, with hands on horn, quite as if he didn't care what happened or what would happen. It wasn't natural, it almost wasn't human. Red, who had been in various sorts of mix-ups and knew all kinds and types of men, had never seen anything like this.

The man gazed at Red a long time, saying nothing, then twisting in the saddle, this way and that, looked down, counting the dead men. He looked at Red again, nodded slightly, and said in a cold, slow, clear voice, "You've done well."

"Whew!" said Red, jabbing a gun into its holster and hastily wiping his sweaty forehead with the palm of his hand. "I thought maybe you were the devil. You gave me an awful scare, coming in so slow and solemn on that black hoss. Almost before the lead had stopped singing."

The man's thin mouth twitched in a vague smile, and he looked at Red with a steady gaze. No man could have told what he thought, though the set of his face and the unwinking steadiness of his eyes made it plain that he *was* thinking. Then he asked in a calm tone, like a man who had the right to know, even to judge. "How'd it happen?"

Red cleared his throat of the smoke's bitter sting, took a full step nearer, stopped, and with an uplifted face, said, "Here's facts, straight as a string. I rode in this afternoon, looking for a job, and loafed over to the Cross Bar Saloon, where I spotted some tinhorns trimming a kid. So I spoke up over the back of my guns, coaxing-like, and they gave him back his money."

"Was Hamel there?" the man asked.

Red's tongue flickered in a pause. In this country, Hamel's seemed a dangerous name. "He was banking, but done as he was told, which was to set tight and keep still," Red said. "I went over to the hotel, but a rip-snorting snorer was bunking in the next room and made sounds like a bucksaw chewing nails. Well, sir, along comes that kid to say he'd overheard the gamblers ribbing up to plug me. Then along comes a little old unwashed runt to say a friend of mine had been hurt and was laying down here at the barn, asking for me. I persuaded him to tell me the truth and I left the kid to keep Shorty company, and came slow and easy down here the back way, crept up close and set with my ears poked out. I don't know *just* what I would have done. Something argumentative, I s'pose. But a long-legged feller come running up, so joyful he was out of breath, to say I'd been plugged with a .38-40 through the window of my room at the hotel. That means they murdered that kid, thinking he was me. So I set about all of a sudden to sort of rectify, as you might say, their wrong notions. I wrecked 'em right, too! But you—you near scared the pea-waddin' out of me, riding in slow and easy like that, like bullets were bees and you were stingproof."

"What's your name?"

"Me, I'm—" Red stopped, struck by a sudden thought. "I'm mostly called Red but I'll answer to the name of Frank Peters."

He figured that the Douglas boy was dead and the wherefore of his coming down to Tajola was veiled under the mysterious instructions of being told to use the name "Frank Peters." So Red thought he might as well monkey with the mystery and see what happened. He did it on impulse, recklessly, somehow vaguely feeling that he was sort of doing the Douglas boy a good turn in taking up the part Douglas had been told to play.

"And you're looking for work?" asked the grim, dark man, calm and cold, but somehow not unfriendly.

"Yessir."

"You're hired, Peters."

The name struck unfamiliarly on Red's ears. He blinked a little, then grinned and asked, "If I don't seem too meddlesome, would you mind telling me what outfit I'm working for?"

"The Zee Zee."

"Ho-lee gosh! Then you're—"

"Monroe."

So this was the man Buck Waxman had said had no friends, just a big pay roll. "A devil in pants," the talkative bartender had called him. Monroe sure looked it, all of it, but in a quiet, tense sort of way. A lot of shooting and numerous dead men strewn about hadn't made him turn a hair.

Red didn't know quite what to say and so stood a little perplexed, half hazily feeling that he wasn't sure he wanted to work for Monroe.

Monroe swung from his horse. There was a quick, smooth litheness about him, and he stood tall and straight. His dark face had a frozen look. His eyes were bright and hard, as if he were used to being a little suspicious of everybody but not afraid of anybody or anything. Just watchful. He dropped the reins and stepped aside.

"Unsaddle my horse," he said. "Water and grain him. Give him a rub and turn him out in the pasture."

"You bet," said Red. Men whom Red worked for always liked the way he jumped to do whatever he was told.

Many a puncher, particularly one who had just gone through such a gunfight, might have had highfalutin notions of his own importance and balked at rubbing down a horse.

In a jiffy Red uncinched the saddle, set it on a

saddle rack, and spread the blankets. He picked brush and currycomb out of the box and led the horse to water. He got a measure of grain, put it into a feed box in the corral. While the horse ate, Red worked busily with currycomb and brush, half whistling, half humming.

Monroe stood by, watching, until Red led out the horse, then he stepped here and there, looking down at the dead men. He had been riding into town and was near the barn when he heard the shooting. He had spurred straight ahead and paused in the open road to see what was going on. Bullets had whizzed near, but neither he nor his gun-trained horse had flinched. It was part of what men called Monroe's "madness" that he never dodged or stepped aside when guns were going off. He seemed to believe he could not be killed, or did not care if he were.

So he had come into the barn before the smoke haze had cleared away. He was surprised to find that one man, and he little more than a lanky youngster, had downed these gunfighters. They were Hamel's men; but Hamel hired a bad lot. So did he himself. So did all the cattlemen of the Tajola range. They were always fighting among themselves over personal grudges. Life was cheap. Monroe's approval was pretty likely to go to the winner—if the fight had been fair.

As Monroe turned he saw an envelope on the ground and half idly stooped. He glanced at the

55

address, frowned, moved nearer a lantern, then stiffened with a startled jerk as if the thing had come to life and bitten him.

Glancing about to make sure he was not being watched, Monroe pulled the letter from the envelope and read. It was the letter the red-headed boy had shown to Red and which Red had unconsciously taken away with him.

Monroe was cold and calm, the least furtive of men, yet it was with a furtive look that he had glanced over his shoulder as he read. The paper rustled faintly from the trembling of his hands as he stared blankly out toward the corral, listening to the faint scrape of currycomb and the half-hummed words of a tuneless song.

With movement of lips as if tasting the words, Monroe muttered, "Jerome Douglas—Jerome!" Then, "Red hair!" This seemed to have a bitter flavor in his mouth, and he added, "It can't be!" But he glanced down at the letter, nodding, mumbling, "Must be." He set his jaws and scowled at nothing, then drew a wallet from his hip pocket and carefully put away the letter. He was troubled. For a time he looked toward the rear of the barn as if half minded to go out there and ask questions. He asked himself the question: "Who could have written it?" But he could give himself no answer. Then he swore under his breath, and it had the sound of a groan clipped by clenched teeth. With downward stroke of fist he muttered noiselessly, "Can't be! Still—maybe." He scowled at the dead men as if they were witnesses that had to be believed, then again protestingly muttered, "Red hair."

Monroe pushed up his hat, breathed hard, wiped sweat off his forehead. "Jerome!" His emotions were going through a sort of rough-and-tumble fight. Then he heard vague, faraway sounds and cocked his head alertly.

There were running feet and breathless, blurting voices as men who had heard the echoes of the shooting came from uptown to learn what had happened.

Monroe stooped quickly, picked up Red's hat, and with long strides went to the back of the barn. Red, with back to the passageway, was stooping low, swishing the brush about the horse's hocks.

Monroe by flip of wrist sent the hat spinning at him. His voice had the snap of command. "Peters! Folks are coming. Get out of sight. I'll see you tomorrow. Uptown. Hunt me up. Remember, you're hired." He faced about, going back into the barn.

Red whistled noiselessly and jumped aside into the shadows, hovering there to listen.

There was a stumble of men's feet at the barn entrance, a shrill chatter of questions, oaths, as the men who had come stopped short, gaping at Monroe.

"No, I didn't do it," Monroe said coldly. "I just

57

heard shooting and come riding up. When I come in 'twas all over. Maybe some of you fellows know what it was over?"

He eyed them questioningly. They shook their heads, mystified. Some wonderingly exchanged half-furtive glances. One fellow ventured, "Maybe some of Morgan's killers nailed 'em." No one echoed that guess. No one felt that it was really a sincere guess, though Morgan and Monroe were enemies.

"Do you reckon," another man suggested, "they got into a quarrel and killed each other off?"

Another blurted, "Naw. These boys, here, was waiting to meet a feller and—"

"And maybe they met him," said Monroe.

"No sir. He didn't come."

"Why not?" asked Monroe sharply. He had a sharp way of dealing with all men.

"'Cause something happened to him uptown."

"We'll all go back uptown," said Monroe.

Red, having heard that much, listened no longer. He slipped quietly away, leaving the corral, again going through the pasture, and in a roundabout way made for the hotel.

CHAPTER 6.

An Old Range Tragedy

Up at the hotel Red saw lamps burning and shadows moving about. The barroom was lighted. If the bartender had shut up shop after Red left, he had been routed out by men who always got thirsty when there was some excitement.

Red peered within. A half dozen men, many of them in undershirts and with tousled hair, stood about with solemn, uneasy air. Their voices reached him in a hesitant grumble, as if they were afraid to talk loud.

Red pushed through and stopped. The bartender's jaw dropped and so did the bottle he was just lifting to the bar. He wasn't entirely sober and shook his head, blinking. "Gosh!" said the bartender; then, staring harder, *"Gosh!"* again, sure that he was looking at a ghost.

Men had turned, eyeing Red.

"Ain't you dead!" one asked in a hushed tone.

"Why, we thought—" another began.

"Yeah, so'd some other folks," said Red, flipping a thumb upward, vaguely indicating the room overhead. "But, like you, they thought wrong. Where's Buck Waxman?"

"He's up there with the doctor. Won't let nobody

see you—or what we thought was you," said a pudgy man who puffed his cheeks as if blowing out the words.

"Have a drink," the bartender offered.

"On me," another urged.

"I'm buying," said a third, slapping palm and coin to the bar.

"I'll be back, maybe," Red answered and went through the barroom.

The pudgy man lifted his voice plaintively. "What could've happened?" Then, accusingly, to the bartender, "Why you told us that—"

"Now, listen. He told me he was going to light out of town. When I heard what happened up there, I thought he'd gone up to get his duds or something . . ."

Upstairs, old Buck Waxman turned in the open door at the sound of feet. His long mustache was as much adroop as if it had been wetted, and he fingered an end of it with twiddling twist of thumb and finger as he peered at Red.

Buck was dressed from hat to boots. His shoulders sagged, and one long arm hung loose as if he didn't know quite what to do with it. He eyed Red with a kind of mournful, staring look.

"Get him?" he asked.

"Get who?"

"Is this a time to be smart-alecky and act stupid?"

"I'm acting natural, like always."

"Didn't you go tearing out of here a while ago after the feller that shot him through the winder?"

"I went tiptoeing out of here a while back down to the corral barn where some folks said you were bad hurt and asking for me."

"Listen, son," said Waxman in a droning, reproachful tone. "That gun going off woke me up. I heard feet running down the hall and came in here and took a look. When I saw it wasn't you, I knew 'twas your feet I'd heard—hopping out to catch 'em. So—"

"Must've been Shorty making his getaway. You see, Buck . . ." Red told the facts fast.

Buck grunted. His face didn't change any more than a printed picture but turned with mournful calm to Red.

"Once I had a little horseshoe affair called a magnet," he said slowly. "You put it down near some iron filings and they'd all come hopping. You're a gosh-blamed magnet when it comes to trouble. Sure as your name is Red Clark, you—"

"Shh! Say, listen, Buck. Something I didn't tell you. I told Monroe my name was Peters, Frank Peters. You see—"

The Adam's apple of Buck's throat bobbed up and down two or three times like a cork when a fish nibbles. He slumped forward a little, peering more closely at Red, then put a hand on Red's arm, holding him as if to make sure he wouldn't get away without answering. "You told him *what?*"

"Frank Peters."

Buck squirmed as if he had a sand burr under his shirt and in a plaintive, anxious tone asked, "How'd you come to do that?"

"I didn't downright say I was Peters. I just said I answered to the name of Peters. I'm particular about lying—sometimes."

"Yeah." Buck's hand dropped from Red's shoulder. "Well, listen. You be gosh-blamed particular now and tell me how you came to call yourself Frank Peters."

Red pointed toward the doorway where the doctor and the wife of the hotel keeper were busy over a body that lay on the bed.

"On account of him, Buck. When I heard that he'd been killed—"

"He ain't killed, quite. But go on—go on."

"Well, I sort of took his name to see what'd happen, because—"

"His name was Smith," said Buck, emphatic.

" 'Tain't. It's Jerome Douglas. But he—"

Buck slowly pushed up his hat and scratched his head hard. Then he reached for a big red bandanna and blew his nose. He turned and looked through the doorway where the old doctor with a whisky-stained nose crouched over the boy while the woman held a lamp for him.

"Let's get out of here," said Buck, interrupting. "Come on. We'll go down and out the back way. Come on." Buck pulled at Red's arm.

"My gosh, Buck. If I didn't know you so blamed well, I'd say you act scared of something."

"You don't know me very blame well if you think I ain't!" stated Buck mournfully. Then with sharp interest, "Did he tell you about that letter he got?"

"He sort of gave it to me and—" Red's hands were moving about his pockets, searching—"and hell! I must've lost it. Stuck it in my pocket when Shorty banged on the door. Gosh, I had it when I started. But now—I sure lost it."

Buck grumbled mournfully and with another pull at Red's arm started off down the hall. They were going as quietly as two thieves when Red, who had a sort of humming in his head from a vague thought that he couldn't quite get hold of, grasped Buck by the shoulder.

"Say!" he exclaimed. "How'd you know there was any letter? He never told nobody but me!"

"I know a lot of things I wish I didn't," said Buck.

They went out to the shanty barn behind the hotel. Buck scratched a match and took up a lantern. Then, silently, he took up his saddle blankets and threw them across the back of his horse.

"What the hell?" said Red. "You riding?"

"I reckon. Seeing as I ain't got wings, I gotta use a horse—me being in a hurry."

"Hurry about what?"

"To get so danged far away from you I can forget what you look like."

"What've I done?" Red eyed him thoughtfully, like a man carefully doing a little sum in addition, such as putting two and two together.

Buck with shambling weave of loose-jointed body reached down the bridle and went to the horse's head, saying nothing.

"'Twas you wrote that letter to him, hunh?" demanded Red.

Buck grunted submissively, then said, with long-drawn shake of head, "I'm never going to try to do anything right again. Here I been coming into town a couple of times a week, looking for young Frank Peters to show up, and he goes and calls himself Smith."

"Who is he? What you running for? Good gosh, Buck, 'tain't like you to be so nervous. Tell me about it. Me, playing I'm him, ain't I got a right to know?"

"You'll learn plenty, pronto, son. Go find that letter. Somebody's sure to find it. It'll be talked about. Monroe'll learn about it, and then—" Buck broke off into a bubble of oaths accompanied by woeful shaking of head.

"My gosh, you act like you had cramps in your belly, Buck."

"I feel that way. Listen. You know the reason I'm near fifty years old? It's 'cause I got discretion. I got a bad case of it right now. If it was catching, like measles, you'd hit your horse and help me kick up some dust."

"Well, tell me some things. What's it all about?"

"All right. You've passed yourself off as Peters, ain't you? Well, just as soon as Monroe gets his eyes on that letter, he's going to inquire around as to who was friendly with this Peters. Who knew him? Who acted like he was laying to meet him? And folks, thinking you are Peters, will up and say, 'Why, old Buck Waxman.' Then Monroe is going to get me in a corner somewheres and say, 'Buck, what call you got to meddle in my affairs?' When Monroe gets folks in a corner, they've got only one way of getting out. That's to dig out after they get buried."

"Aw shucks! You can't make me believe you're scared of any damn man, Buck."

"I'm in a bad hole, son. Bad. Y'see, I sort of like Monroe. He's a devil. If him and Old Nick got into a row, Old Nick would go limping off with a sore tail, a-hunting beefsteak to put on his eye. But I've known him a long time, me and my brother, both. He's never talked intimate to me but he has to my brother Bill. And Bill has talked to me. That's where I got the notion to bring that kid down here and let Monroe get to liking him without knowing he was liking his own son."

"*What!*" said Red, making much the same sort of movement as if he'd sat on a tack.

"Yeah. Y'see, twenty years ago, or just about,

65

Monroe got some damn fool notions. I, personal, suspect Hamel gave 'em to him. Y'see, his hair is as black as the inside of a deep hole in a thunderstorm. Mrs. Monroe's hair was brown. She was a mighty fine woman. Pretty as a picture and proud as Punch. Monroe was awful jealous. One day he came back out from town looking black and a little drunk. Her and him had a talk together in the house. Sort of loud, his voice was. I was setting out behind the kitchen, washing some old chaps with saddle soap. She came out tall and straight and pale, holding the kid up close. She says to me, 'Buck, take me to town.' So I ties a pair of broncs to the buckboard, and off we go— her without a stitch of clothes but what she had on her back. We go along in silence for a couple of miles, then she says, 'Buck, could you let me have some money?'

" 'Me, I got less'n four bits,' I says. ' 'Bout how much was you wanting, Mrs. Monroe?' She says, ' 'Bout fifty dollars'll do. I'm going back to Colorado.' I says, 'I'll get it in town.' Then she set there staring at that kid's red hair, just staring and staring. After a while she says, 'Buck, do you know Diamond Jack O'Brien?' He was a flashy red-headed gambler in town that used bottle-stink. I says, 'Yeah, I've smelled him.'

"In town I takes her over to the boarding house—we didn't have a hotel then—to wait stage time. Then I goes to the express office and I says

66

to the manager, 'I want to borrow fifty dollars.' He says, 'No,' but takes a couple more looks at me and kind of weakens, gets polite and asks, 'What's the matter?' I explain that a friend of mine is leaving town and needs the money and that if I ain't hung for using unmannerly means of getting it, I'll sure pay it back. So he gives it to me. Then I goes up to the Red Star joint, walks in, and asks casual-like, 'Where is Diamond Jack?' Folks look at me funny-like. Then I hear that Monroe has shot him. Most folks seem to think Monroe done right. Me, too—for a time.

"Then one day me and Oliver Morgan has a talk. In them days Morgan and Monroe wasn't unfriendly. And he says to me, 'Buck, now that Diamond Jack is dead, Hamel is sort of the whole show, ain't he?' I admits it. Then he says, 'I always had a suspicion that Hamel was afraid of Diamond Jack. Leastwise, we all know that Jack wasn't afraid of Hamel. Fellows used to josh Diamond Jack about being the only red-headed man in the country, and he used to play up to 'em by winking and looking wise. He was bad stuck on himself. Yeah. And, Buck, I guess if the truth was known, Hamel didn't care about the damage he'd do to a good woman like Mrs. Monroe if he could just make somebody mad enough to kill Jack—get him out of the way.' What old Oliver Morgan said made me mighty thoughtful."

Red nodded in complete understanding, yet

inquired with puzzlement, "How come a man like Monroe is thick with a gazebo like Hamel?"

Buck sighed mournfully. "Monroe is bullheaded and in some ways—most ways—an awful fool. If he trusts a man, why then he seems to feel it's what you call aspersions on himself if you try to show him the man ain't fit to be trusted. He ain't got no great personal liking for Hamel. He ain't got no great personal liking for anybody, except maybe my brother Bill. But Hamel for twenty year has sung the tune, 'Mr. Monroe, folks is down on me 'cause I'm your friend.' So Monroe says, 'I'll show folks they'd better let my friends alone.' He's helped Hamel get to be a rich man, rich cowman. He's lent him money. He's fought fights for him out on the range and here in town. Hamel has got all swelled up and he wouldn't know how to be honest if he tried.

"Listen. Once I knew a man that had a pet coyote. He'd raised him from a teeny-weeny pup. He gave him all he could eat and made him a pet. Well, sir, that coyote, being a coyote, would sneak out and kill the man's chickens. He got so he'd even go out and bring in other coyotes; and once when the feller was away, they got into the corral and killed some calves. That feller would never believe it was his coyote which'd come around and lick his hand like a dog. So me, havin' a suspicious instinct about coyotes, I laid for him. Sorta proved things to the feller, which is that you can't make a coyote fat so he'll quit being a coyote. I got similar sentiments about Hamel. You can't make him so rich and fat he'll quit being a dirty sneak. Personally, I think he hates Monroe because he's afraid of him and because he knows everybody in this part of the country feels Monroe is the big man. Hamel wants to be the big man himself.

"I'll tell you some more quick, then I got to ride. And if you want to be sensible, you'll keep leg to leg with me. Monroe's losing cows. Rustler. Sometimes his men get killed, mysterious. Times are bad. Hamel and other folks try to make out that old Oliver Morgan is doing it. All right. My brother Bill coaxed Monroe into hiring a couple of detectives from the cowmen's association to come here and nose about. They came, and a couple hours later they were dead. Who done it? I been gosh almighty curious. You come with me, now, out on the range and we'll monkey around and see what we can learn."

"But what about that boy in the hotel?" asked Red. "He's Monroe's son, ain't he? He's near dead, ain't he? You got him down here in this pickle, Buck, and now when he's bad hurt, are you going off and leave him without friends?"

"If he don't kick the bucket, he'll be took care of. Y'see, Monroe never spoke of his wife from the day she left. He's the sort of feller that, if he gets an idea, won't let go. He'd almost rather be in the wrong than weak enough to change his mind or admit that maybe he'd made a mistake. But he has talked some in recent years to my brother Bill about the boy. Monroe believes in blood and breed. It shows in his cows, in his horses, and in his men. He used to say to Bill that he'd like to get hold of the boy and put him over the jumps just to see if the kid had the right stuff in him. He was always wondering if this kid had the fighting heart that a Monroe ought to have. Without saying nothing to nobody, I just thought I'd get the kid down here and edge him into a job on the Zee Zee. The kid didn't know who his dad was 'cause when Mrs. Monroe sent me back that fifty dollars, she said from now on her name was Mrs. Douglas, like before she was married, and that little Jerry was to be brought up to think his dad was dead. She said there was some property coming to her which would be given to the kid when he was twenty-one, and she was going to have him educated like a gentleman. And she asked would I always remember her and, if I had a chance, kind of keep an eye on the boy. Yeah. I played hell, and you helped me! You riding with me?"

"No, I'm not. That boy took a slug in his back that was meant for me, and—"

"All right, all right," Buck said hastily. "Have it your way. Instinct tells me when I ought to run. You're going to catch billy-hell, but I reckon old

Monroe won't shoot you on sight like he'd come near doing to me when he learns what I've done. You can tell him the truth. That boy up there is his son. 'By. I'm on my way but maybe I won't run as far as some folks think. An old man like me don't stand traveling like younger folks."

Buck brought out his horse, thrust a loose arm toward Red, shaking hands, then with a quick, nimble swing got into the saddle and loped off through the starlit shadows before Red could ask any more questions. And Red's tongue fairly squirmed with questions that he would have liked to ask.

He watched Buck vanish into the dim night, then shook his head. "He ain't running. Not because he's scared. He's just going some place. And maybe if I had some sense, I'd be going some place, too."

CHAPTER 7.

A Night's Rest for Red

Red didn't want to talk to anybody in the hotel barroom. He didn't want to talk to anybody anywhere. He wanted to think. He had a strong impulse to run back up the stairs and ask the gray doctor with the red nose if Jerome Douglas was going to live. Merely asking the question wouldn't help the boy, yet asking such questions when a man was hurt or sick was the only way of showing you were his friend.

Red thought that about the most sensible thing he could do, when it came daylight, would be to go over his tracks down at the corral and see if he could pick up the letter he had lost out of his pocket. If he could get his hands on it, then everything would be pretty well straightened out again. At least, nobody would ever know that old Buck Waxman had been meddling in Monroe's affairs.

Red saw a light in the hotel kitchen and the shadow of a woman moving about. Mrs. Wyman, the wife of the man who owned the hotel, was busy poking up a fire.

She was a lanky woman who frowned a good deal and worked hard. Her voice was harsh and her hands were hard; she didn't like loafers and thought that her husband was too much like one, but she was a good woman.

Red knocked at the screen door, and she looked up calmly. Mrs. Wyman wasn't skittish. She didn't jump if she saw a mouse or if strange men knocked on the door at three o'clock in the morning.

She was standing in the light and couldn't see well, so she came toward the door, peering hard.

"Ho, *you.*" Then with a rush of words, she said, "I can't really blame you for getting shot at, but I wish to the Lord it'd been somewheres else than in my hotel. Where's Buck Waxman? Monroe just sent word for Buck to come and see him at the Cross Bar, and I reckon he'd better get over there. Where is he? Do you know?"

"Buck had some business that took him out of town, Mrs. Wyman." Red began to feel that maybe Buck's instinct was a pretty reliable guide. "I just wanted to ask how is the boy?"

"How is he? How is he?" She stood tall and scornful. "How'd anybody be with a hole in him *that* big?" She held up a bony fist. "The doctor took out a chunk of lead that big—or nearly. You and him brothers?"

"No'm. But we're friends. Is there anything I can do?"

Mrs. Wyman made a snorting sound and dipped her finger into the water that was heating on the stove. "Men can't do nothing around sick folks. Most helpless critters on earth, men is."

"Anything I *can* do, Mrs. Wyman. I'll see as how you get paid for—"

"Shut up. I'm tending to the boy the very best I can. Times are hard, but I ain't got to the place yet where I have to have pay for nursing folks that are hurt. Such a nice boy he looks. Much handsomer than you—" her glance seemed to be making comparison between Red's features and those of the wounded boy—"which is why I thought maybe you wasn't brothers."

Red grinned. "Yes'm. You're right. I never

won no prizes on my good looks. But now in a flapjack-eating contest!"

"I don't know what this country is coming to!" She dipped her finger again into the water which was heating slowly. "Somebody told me a while ago there'd been an awful killing down at the Stage barn."

"Yeah?" Red inquired, interested.

"Old Monroe was standing there when folks heard the shots and come. But he pretended he didn't do it. Yet he's about the only man in this country that could shoot three or four men and not get hit himself. I told you he'd sent for Buck Waxman, didn't I? They were Hamel's friends down there at the barn, so *of course* Monroe didn't do it. No. Hum!"

Plainly she did not like Monroe, or Hamel, either.

She poked more wood into the fire and without looking up said, "You'd better get out of town. Them gamblers'll kill you."

"You think so, Mrs. Wyman?"

"Well, who do you think shot that boy through my window? They mistook him for you, didn't they?"

"'Pears like somebody did make a little mistake."

"You talk like you was glad 'twas him instead of you that got shot."

Red shifted his feet and wet his lips but couldn't

74

think of anything to reply. That was the way with women. They said things in such a way that you couldn't answer back without laying yourself wide open to more reproaches.

"I reckon I'd better be going," said Red.

"Where?"

"Don't know, exactly."

Mrs. Wyman dipped her finger into the water. "Nearly hot," she said. "The doctor wants it. Now you—" she went with long, quick strides across the kitchen and flung open a door—"bed down in here. It's where the cook sleeps—when we have a cook. I won't tell anybody I saw you. Let folks think you've rode off, which you should have done. What you staying for, anyhow?"

"Who, me? Well, ma'am, I'll tell you. I'm a little curious about what's going to happen next. It's a weakness with me, like whisky is with some folks."

Mrs. Wyman looked at him with rather friendly eyes. She nodded as if deciding, then said, "Why don't you ride over to Oliver Morgan's and get a job? They're nice folks, the Morgans. Not like some people. In having trouble with Hamel, maybe you'll get Monroe down on you. He's a holy terror, Mr. Monroe!" She dropped her voice. "I'm going to send word to Mrs. Morgan and ask her to take that poor hurt boy over to her place. They are mighty nice folks, the Morgans. Not like some!"

"Listen, ma'am. Doesn't anybody ever stand up to Monroe?"

"No, they don't. Seems like he ain't human. Everybody's afraid of him, and he ain't afraid of nothing. He's a mean man, Monroe is. Mean. 'Pears like nobody can kill him. 'Pears like bullets just won't touch him. The only good thing about him is them Waxman boys, Bill and Buck. He'll halfway listen to them. Mrs. Morgan tells me that if it hadn't been for the Waxmans there'd have been open war on the range long ago between Monroe and the Morgans. You get to bed. The doctor's waiting for this water. Good night."

She shut the door upon Red, leaving him in the dark. He struck a match and glanced about but did not light the lamp. He kicked off his clothes, down to his underwear, and got into the bunk. He felt that he was not going to be able to sleep because there was so much to think about, but it seemed that he had just closed his eyes when there was a pounding on the door.

"Yeah?" he called. It was broad daylight, more than daylight. The sun was high.

Mrs. Wyman opened the door and peered in. She looked tired and a little excited. She had not been to bed, for as soon as young Douglas had been tended to and left, only half conscious, to rest, it had been time to start breakfast.

"Hurry and get into your clothes. I got a stack of flapjacks and 'lasses. Eat, then light out of town.

Monroe is in the bar asking for you and waiting. You don't wanta meet him. Come, hurry and eat. I had a fellow go down and get your horse. It'll be out back by the time you've eaten."

Red grinned and thanked her with, "Now that's fine!" He liked to have folks like him, particularly gaunt, hard-working Western women. It made him feel that he must be a pretty good sort, because such women were wary judges of human nature.

Red dressed, went out back and washed with much splashing and rubbing, sat at a kitchen table, and gobbled flapjacks and drank coffee. Mrs. Wyman looked on approvingly. The way Red ate made her know that he thought her flapjacks were good and it made her know, too, that he wasn't the kind to get scared and lose his appetite because a man like Monroe was looking for him.

"You light out over to the Morgans," Mrs. Wyman urged.

Red popped spoonful after spoonful of sugar into a fresh cup of coffee, stirred it thoughtfully, and shook his head.

"No, ma'am, Monroe don't mean to do anything to me."

"Don't you go trusting him!"

Red reached into his pocket for money. "How much?"

"You having to sleep in the cook's bunk and eating in the kitchen, I ought not to charge. But you can give me four bits if you want."

"The bed was soft and the flapjacks sweet, the way I like 'em." Red clicked down two dollars. "That kind of special attention makes me happy to pay."

Mrs. Wyman reluctantly fingered the money, then put it on a high shelf. "I'll get some port wine for him." Her hand flipped upward vaguely. "The doctor said it might do him good."

Red fumbled again in his pocket. There was the faint clink of metal as he felt about, selecting what he wanted. Then with a quick upward reach he put something on the shelf and went out the kitchen door.

Mrs. Wyman watched him, then turned and hastily felt on the shelf. She thought there were three dollars, but one seemed heavy and slick. She gathered them into her palm and looked. One was a twenty-dollar gold piece.

CHAPTER 8.

Red Versus Hellbender

Monroe stood at the end of the bar with a glass of whisky before him, saying nothing. He was tall and straight with quick eyes that went squarely to men's faces and searched them. Some men turned their backs to him and tried to pretend they did not know he was there. His presence made conversation awkward. Monroe was not quarrelsome, but there was an air of menace about him. For the most part men moved quietly and spoke in low tones whenever Monroe stood watching. It was generally thought that he was a little crazy but not noisy, like most fellows who had a touch of loco.

Red came in with shambling scrape of spurs, paused at the doorway, and looked about. He walked straight up to Monroe, who eyed him piercingly from under a scrutinizing frown, appraising him intently.

"Word's come you wanted to see me, Mr. Monroe."

Monroe said nothing. He thought that he was looking at his son, or a boy he wanted to believe was his son. The men who stood about, shifting their feet, half-furtively peered at them. Monroe's jaws were locked. His dark eyes went up and down Red's body and fastened finally on his face. He could not believe this boy was his son. He did not look like a Monroe or a Douglas; yet men, gunmen, were being put away over on the sandhill, and that was what happened when men went up against a Monroe or a Douglas.

Red's eyes were blue and direct. They glowed and gleamed with downright honesty. His wide mouth had a good-natured twitch. Monroes or Douglases had not been people who smiled much. This redhead wore two guns and had a catlike suppleness of body, all sinew and lean muscle. Monroe believed that blood ran true to breed. A fighting heart never came from weakling sire or dam. But, after all, a gunfight was rather like a gamble. He had seen fellows who didn't have downright grit get cornered and, with luck, shoot their way out. Rats bit terriers and got away.

Now if Red had known that Monroe had that letter, he very likely would have up and told him the whole story. But he didn't know it and not wanting to drag in Buck Waxman and give away Buck's secrets, Red stood fast, rolled a cigarette, and waited.

Monroe, in turn, was wondering if Red knew, or believed, that he was Monroe's son. He did not think so. Monroe had very readily guessed from what he had learned and because he knew Waxman's handwriting, that Buck Waxman had sent for the boy. But Buck Waxman was a close-mouthed fellow—and honest. So Monroe was really not as angry as he tried to feel toward Buck.

Monroe's deepest and most earnest thought was, "I've got to make him show me what's inside of him. If he's got a yellow spot as big as a dime hid away, I'll bring it out."

He said coldly, "Where the hell you been? Keeping me waiting!"

Red, with the unlighted cigarette at his lips and a match on its way, paused. He shook the match out and dropped it. With a twitch of his lips he spat out the cigarette.

"Mr. Monroe, us being strangers, I reckon you don't know about my sentiments. I'm not used to being cussed—'cept when I got it coming."

"Meaning?" Monroe inquired with a deepening frown.

"Just that," said Red softly with a slight nod and with eyes that met and held the hard look of menace glowing in Monroe's.

Men who saw and heard wriggled uneasily, getting nearer the doorways, casting glances toward the shelter offered under tables. But nothing happened—or rather something amazing did happen. That is, Monroe did nothing. He said simply, "Let's take a walk, Peters."

"Yessir. But if you don't mind, would you call me Red? Most folks do. I'm more used to it."

On the instant Monroe's eyes lighted with an ominous gleam. "Red" was a name that he didn't want to hear or use. He understood that "Frank Peters," being a recently assumed name, wasn't as yet quite familiar, and Red couldn't instinctively answer when he heard it.

"I'll call you by the name you gave me, Peters," said Monroe.

"Fair enough," Red admitted, feeling that the joke was pretty much on himself and really wanting to grin a little. One did not easily grin in Monroe's presence.

Monroe started out, and Red went with him. Men stared with questioning eyes, not understanding. This boy, so to speak, had slapped Hamel good and hard in the face, and had stood up to Monroe himself. Now the two of them were going off together, taking a walk. When Monroe had something to settle with a man, he did not take him off to one side or out for a walk. He settled it wherever they chanced to meet, quickly.

Monroe led the way around back of the hotel where a saddled horse stood. The animal flicked up its ears as it glanced toward Red.

"Your horse?" Monroe asked.

"Mine."

"Were you getting ready to ride some place?"

"All the notion of riding I've had in mind is wherever you send me," said Red.

"Yes. But you'll ride the horse I give you," Monroe answered. "Men who work for me take what comes, and I have a preference for them that stay in the saddle."

"Lots of times I didn't stay," said Red. "There's no horse but some man can ride him and no man but some horse can spill him. Being lucky, I'm fair to middling. Leastways, I never yet lit on the back of my neck, though coming down on the seat of my pants was bad enough. I'm too skinny, and my bones rattle when I hit."

Monroe eyed him, scarcely knowing whether he did not like, or liked very much, this good-natured kind of chatter. At least, it showed that the boy had good nerves and didn't brag. Monroe detested nervous men and loathed braggers.

Red saw Mrs. Wyman's anxious face peering from the back door. When she went away, he had the feeling that she was still watching without being seen.

Monroe walked around to one side of the shed, pointed to an overturned bucket, and said, "Set down, Peters."

Red sat down. Monroe, with thumbs in belt and hat pushed back, leaned against a post of the shed and looked at him.

"Now tell me again, and carefully, just what happened last night from the time you hit town," he said.

Red told him, fairly and honestly, with one exception. He made no mention of the letter and so concealed the identity of Jerome Douglas. He concealed, too, Buck Waxman's confession. He told of meeting Waxman and all about that. Monroe got the idea that Waxman had not yet disclosed the information that he had written the letter and so brought young Jerome Douglas down to Tajola. Perhaps Buck had wanted to try the boy out first himself. That Red admitted having known Buck before and elsewhere seemed reasonable enough to Monroe. Buck would likely have moved about the country and made a point of meeting, looking over, sort of studying the boy he believed was Monroe's son. Monroe was exasperated at Buck's trick but not really angry about it.

So Monroe did not try to trip Red up or press him to tell about the things he was plainly concealing.

"Now," said Monroe, "we'll walk some more. Come with me."

Red was a tall boy but he did not come more than shoulder high to Monroe, who carried himself straight and had square shoulders. He held his head high in a stiff-necked sort of way.

Together he and Red went tramping up the street, much like two strangers who happened to be going in the same direction. Folks who saw them turned to watch.

Near the corner of the General Store, Monroe stopped and pointed. "See the blacksmith shop over yonder? You go over there and wait till I come."

Red went over to the shop where a big man with bare, hairy arms was shaping horseshoes. A scrubby little Mexican boy tugged at the bellows.

A fine-looking, powerful horse with roving wild eyes was tied to a post near the blacksmith shop.

"Howdy," said Red.

Blackie looked up. "So you're him, hunh?"

"Enough like him not to argue about it," said Red agreeably.

Blackie looked from Red to the horse and back

again. Then he shoved the horseshoe into the coals and swore at the little Mexican, who began to pump briskly. Then putting his two great calloused hands on his hips, he glared at Red.

"So you think you can ride Hellbender, hunh?" the blacksmith asked with a kind of menacing jeer.

Red turned squarely about and looked at the horse with new interest. A powerful beast, long of leg, deep-chested, thin of flank. Hellbender had a well-shaped head and a wiry neck, but was wall-eyed and nervous, a man-hater. So this was what Monroe was going to put him up against.

"Yours?" Red asked.

"Mine," said Blackie and reaching up to a shelf, he took down a small canvas bag and dropped it with a metallic clank on the anvil. "I got me three hundred dollars, gold, right here, that says you can't ride him. There'll be other fellers down here with as much or more to bet the same. He's killed better men than you'll ever be. That horse ain't never been rode. He ain't never going to be but once, neither. The day he is, I kill him!"

Red grunted.

"What you mean by that *unh?*" The blacksmith imitated the grunt, glowering.

Red eyed the big, dark, bad-tempered black-smith. "Did you eat something that didn't agree with you, or what?" he asked.

"Don't get funny! Don't get funny!" Blackie

warned, growling far down in his throat and frowning.

"It's you that's acting funny. Danged funny. But somehow I don't feel like laughing much. What are you riled up about? You trying to throw a scare into me so I won't get on that horse?"

"If you got good sense, you won't." The blacksmith added ominously, "When you get throwed, he'll tromp on you."

Red looked the horse over carefully.

"Monroe must have it in for you," said the blacksmith. "That's why he had me bring up this horse. He's never been rode."

"Yeah, and you've worked careful to make a killer out of what was born a good horse."

The blacksmith jiggled the little canvas bag, rattling his money. "You going to bet you can ride him? Here's three hundred dollars."

"I ain't strong enough to carry around such a lot of money as all that. It weighs you down, makes you unhappy. You just can't be happy till you get rid of it. Leastwise, I can't."

The blacksmith snorted, put the canvas bag back on the shelf, took down a bottle of whisky, gulped a time or two, swore at the little Mexican, fished out the red-hot horseshoe, and began to hammer.

Soon after, a man came riding slowly from town. His horse, a beautiful roan, came along as if half asleep, head down and feet almost dragging. The man in the saddle was lean, loose-jointed, and round-shouldered, and rode as if he had no backbone.

Red called out impulsively, "Why, hello there, Buck," before he realized that this was not old Buck Waxman but somebody who looked mighty like him.

The horseman without a flickering change of expression in his face rode right up to where Red was standing and looked down with keen narrow eyes that peered from a face full of wrinkles.

He spoke with a slow, monotonous drawl. "Don't be calling me no insulting names. All my life I've been mistook for that damn fool, which, seeing how ugly he is, is sure hard on my self-respect."

"Oh, then you're Bill Waxman?"

There was not a twitch of expression on the Zee Zee foreman's face. He peered with keen gray eyes at Red, looking straight into his face for a long time. Old Bill was not quite sure what to think. Monroe had told him everything and had showed him the letter. Red did not look quite like old Bill thought a son of Monroe should look, but he did look range-born and bred; and the foreman of the Zee Zee was a good judge of men.

"So your name's Peters?"

Red nodded. Somehow he felt it was less like telling a lie if he just nodded instead of speaking.

"Are you much good at riding broncs, son?"

"I've set on a few."

Old Bill eyed him with moody scrutiny, then said, "Be honest with me, son, and speak up truthful. It's more important than you think. If you're not as good as any man that ever hugged leather with his legs, up and say so. Mr. Monroe'll forgive you for being sensible enough not to try—yeah, a whole lot sooner'n he'd forgive you for getting throwed. 'Tain't no disgrace not to climb a horse. Now me, I wouldn't climb that horse for a thousand dollars. He'd break my old bones like a bull going through a brush pile. But it's a powerful disgrace, after you've climbed a horse, not to stay there."

There was a sort of kindliness in old Bill's low voice that warmed Red's heart.

"Maybe I won't ride him, Mr. Waxman, but if I don't, you'll say a good job of trying was done."

Old Bill took his time about replying, and all the while his keen gray eyes were peering searchingly at Red's face.

Then he said, "If you get on that horse, you stay there. No matter how, you stay there. Don't you come off. Mr. Monroe is one mighty queer man."

"Blackie over there says he's never been ridden."

Old Bill took his time about answering. He looked toward the blacksmith shop, toward the horse, back at Red. "I reckon that's right," he said. "Only the reasons that have caused some men to get throwed ain't going to apply none to you. I'm having a man bring down your horse and saddle. There ain't going to be no grease smeared on your saddle blankets. And if your cinch busts, it won't be because somebody nicked it with a knife."

Old Bill swung off his horse and dropped the reins. With shambling gait he went to the blacksmith shop.

The blacksmith called out heartily and with much respect, " 'Lo there, Bill. How are you? Come down to see Hellbender kick the dust in that galoot's face? Haw haw haw! Say, was Mr. Monroe joking when he said he halfway believed he had a young feller that could ride him?"

Old Bill, not answering, leaned against a post.

Blackie thrust the cold horseshoe back into the coals and reached down his bag of dollars, making them clink.

"Three hundred dollars—that's what I'm betting."

"Sack full of washers," said old Bill.

"Washers! Nosir! Look here!" The blacksmith opened the bag and held out the gold.

"Three hundred dollars," Bill mused, eyeing the horse, then looking across to Red. "Hmm. I'll take it."

"You?"

"Sure."

"Put up or shut up," said the blacksmith aggressively. He didn't much like betting against old Bill, who was a smart man.

"Ain't my word good?" Bill inquired mildly

with a pinpoint sort of light in his old gray eyes.

"Well—er—yes—but—" Blackie wanted to hedge. Maybe, after all, this kid was a good rider; and if Bill Waxman was backing him, there wouldn't be any chance to play tricks. "Of course, Bill, if you know the kid, why then maybe I'd better keep my money in my pocket."

"I never laid eyes on him before. But I took your bet."

"You never laid eyes—Then how do you know who he is?" The blacksmith was confused, also a little suspicious. He didn't dare even remotely hint that maybe old Bill was not telling the truth. For a mild man, Bill could be amazingly disagreeable.

"Mr. Monroe hired him." Old Bill said no more.

The blacksmith took down his bottle of whisky and offered it. Old Bill shook his head. The blacksmith threw back his head and gurgled.

Red squatted down, off to one side, and eyed the powerful Hellbender.

"I don't feel happy," said Red to himself. "I'm what you call an imposticator, or something. That name Peters don't set right. It's true I *have* been thrown. But a lot of times I haven't been, too. A nice dab of glue on the seat of my britches might come in handy."

CHAPTER 9.

A Certain Gang Lays Low

When Monroe left Red on the street, he had gone on down to the Cross Bar Saloon where his foreman, old Bill, was sitting on the sidewalk with his back against the building. Old Bill commanded about as much respect as any man on the range and had less dignity. He was a lonely, modest, retiring old codger, watchful as a hawk and quiet as a sulky Indian.

"Learned anything?" Monroe had asked.

"Nothing," said old Bill. "But if Hamel didn't put those fellows up to it last night, I reckon they calculated he wouldn't tear none of his hair out when he learned what they'd done. Hamel is going to be plumb fuzzled, Mr. Monroe, wondering why you're all het up over a shooting scrape here in town when there's been dozens before and nothing much said."

"This is different, Bill. The boy's horse is up back of the hotel. Have it taken down to the blacksmith shop and go on down yourself. Maybe last night he was just lucky in that gunfight. But there's no luck in riding an outlaw. I'm going to see what kind of a heart he's got. If he quits, gets thrown, shows yellow—well—to hell with him!"

"Well, I been throwed and so've you. We've managed to hold our heads up in the community some, anyhow."

"This is different. Different, because—Bill, if he rides that horse to a standstill, you want to know what I'll do?"

"Yeah."

"I'm going over to Judge Tiller and make a will. I'll know the boy's a real Monroe!"

Bill had solemnly scratched an ear as he watched Monroe turn and go through the wide double doors of the Cross Bar Saloon. Then he had raised his hand, and a wiry young puncher with a thin, hard face and eyes like beads came at a jog trot from across the street. He was a bad one, this half-breed Sam, but he had a doglike affection for both the Waxmans and especially for old Bill.

"Sam, you ride up back of the hotel. There's a horse there, saddled. You switch saddles. Understand? Then you ride down to the blacksmith shop. You ride the stranger's saddle and you set in it till I come over and tell you to get down. Understand?"

The half-breed shrugged and grinned.

Monroe walked into the Cross Bar Saloon and stopped short. It was a wide room and seemed dim to anybody who entered from the bright sunshine outside. There were many men standing about, some of them Hamel's riders.

92

Monroe scarcely glanced at them. He spoke to the bartender. "Where's Hamel?"

"Hamel? Oh, he ain't come down yet, Mr. Monroe. Still asleep. Do I call him for you?"

"No," said Monroe. He started back through the long barnlike saloon.

His back was no sooner turned than the bartender took up a slender stick about eight feet long. When Monroe had passed from sight, the bartender began thumping the ceiling: *tap-tap-tap-tap-tap-tap-tap-tap.* He paused, looking up, waiting. From overhead, faintly, there came slow answering taps.

"What's that little game, Slim?" a man inquired.

"Oh, I was just letting the boss know he was about to have a visitor. One he ain't anxious to see, neither."

"Is there liable to be trouble?" a man asked in a low voice, leaning well over the bar.

The bartender eyed the man with an expressionless stare, then slowly winked.

"He's just got everybody bluffed, that's all," said another man, looking in the direction Monroe had gone.

Monroe went up the back stairs and along a dim, dusty, narrow hall where there were rooms for private games of poker and some with bunks in them to stow away drunks.

Up near the front of the hall Monroe struck on a door.

"Yeah?" Hamel answered. "Who is it?"

For answer, Monroe shook the latch against its bolt.

"Oh, you," said Hamel. "Just a minute, Mr. Monroe, till I get my pants on."

"Never mind your pants."

When Hamel opened the door, he was slipping suspenders up on his shoulders and his hair was tousled, and he tried to blink as if he had just awakened.

Monroe strode in with a quick glance all about. He turned a straight-backed chair around, straddled it, and sat down, folding his arms on the back. He looked up steadily at Hamel.

Hamel was fat and blowzy, with sagging jaws and dark, crafty eyes. In some ways he was a smart fellow, up to all sorts of nimble trickery, but right now he was uneasy. His gun and belt were hanging over the back of a chair within easy reach but they might as well have been a mile away for any move that he would make for them in Monroe's presence. It would have been just like backing up to a husky Missouri mule and trying to out-kick him.

"Hamel, did you send Crawley up to that fellow's room at the hotel last night?"

"Never!" said Hamel, looking amazed.

"Where is Crawley?"

"Hell fire, I don't know. Isn't he down at the barn?"

"If so, would I be here asking where he is?"

"Who says I sent Crawley up there? Did Crawley go and tell any such story? Wait till I get my hands on that drunken runt. What's this all about, Mr. Monroe?"

"Where are those two gamblers?"

"I wish I knew." Hamel sounded indignant. "They lit out last night right after that poker game. If I'd suspicioned they were cheating, I sure would've fixed 'em. If there's anything I hate, it's a cheating gambler. You know *that,* Mr. Monroe."

"You're a damn fool!" said Monroe coldly. "You're as crooked as a dog's hind leg, Hamel. You've stolen right and left from the county all these years. Most politicians do. I've backed you up because you're no worse than anybody else would have been. I've put up with a lot from you, Hamel, and—"

"And I've always been your friend, Mr. Monroe."

"Yes, friendly enough to tell me what my enemies have been up to. And you've been damn well paid. But if I ever get the notion that you have anything to do with shooting men in the back, I'll kill you, Hamel."

Hamel's knees trembled, but with all the intonation of amazement he blurted, "Whatever can you mean?"

"I mean somebody sent Crawley up to that boy's room last night—"

"I never. S'help me God, I didn't. Somebody

95

may have told Crawley that I sent word for him to go, but I never. I didn't know a thing about it. You ask Crawley. Just ask him."

"I will when I find him. Also, it was your Cross Bar men that were laying for that boy down at the barn."

"Those gamblers must've hired 'em. I didn't know a thing about it. The gamblers were awful het up against that red-headed feller. Who the hell is he, anyhow?"

"I don't know," said Monroe grimly. "But I'm going to find out something about him this morning. I'm putting him on Hellbender."

"Then he's no friend of yours?" Hamel exclaimed with a loose wobble of his thick lips. He sounded relieved. "But old Buck Waxman knew him." Somehow, Hamel seemed to accuse Buck Waxman of knowing too much. "I wonder, can he be a detective?"

"In which case," said Monroe coldly, "it wouldn't appear to be Oliver Morgan who shot those detectives."

"Don't you ever believe it wasn't. That old hide stealer is tricky, Mr. Monroe. He's got friends setting here in town right under our noses. He don't want his doings looked into. I tell you, Mr. Monroe, the Morgans are still trying to shoot you—in the back."

Monroe's lips tightened and his eyes gleamed. About three years before, in this same Cross Bar

Saloon, Hamel had emptied a shotgun into a half-drunken stranger who, with both guns out, had risen up to take a shot at Monroe's back. That and other things, scattered over a period of twenty years, had made Monroe feel that Hamel was pretty much his friend. Hamel made out that he knew this drunken stranger had been hired by Oliver Morgan to kill Monroe. Monroe had never quite believed that. He had been having trouble with the Morgans. He appeared always to be having trouble with the Morgans; but as much as he hated the tribe, he could not quite believe that Oliver Morgan would hire somebody to murder him.

Some people, talking privately among themselves, had said it was queer that Hamel, who wasn't quick with any sort of gun, should have had a shotgun handy just at the big moment. Some—though they never let Monroe know of it—said they halfway suspected that the stranger had been a man Hamel wanted to get rid of and so had been put up by Hamel to try to kill Monroe. Some people didn't put any low-down dirty trick above Hamel.

"I've sure been your friend, ain't I, Mr. Monroe?" Hamel asked, looking humble and abused. He knew that gratitude was Monroe's weakest spot.

Monroe stood up and pushed the chair aside. "Yes, and I've been yours."

"I hope you still are and always will be, Mr. Monroe."

Monroe growled vaguely. He did not like Hamel, had never liked him, but somehow had always felt indebted to him.

"Was it you, Mr. Monroe, that wiped out them men down to the barn last night?"

"Since when do you think I've taken to lying?"

"Oh, I never meant that, Mr. Monroe."

"I said I rode in and found them dead. If you want me to feel you're as innocent as you appear, Hamel, you'd better bring me those gamblers' ears—with their scalps. That'll be all for now."

Monroe turned and went out, slamming the door.

Hamel stared at the door, then went near it with head bent, listening to the tap of Monroe's boots as he strode down the hallway.

A door from the next room opened behind him, and Hamel turned about, facing the gamblers and little, shivering Shorty Crawley.

"We heard!" said Perley Price.

The younger of the gamblers, who had a wolf face and was known as Timkins, snarled, "You sure piled it on us, didn't you? Here's my ears—do you want to try to take them to him!"

Crawley was snuffling and whimpering like a dog that had been kicked for obeying orders.

"Now, now, boys." Hamel puffed unhappily. "I was in a tight hole. I got us all out, didn't I?"

"Yeah," said wolf-faced Timkins. "You knuckled

down to him like a scared kid before a teacher."

"With him out of the way," said Perley Price, "you could run this damn country yourself, any old way you wanted."

"What's going to become of me?" Shorty Crawley whimpered.

"Now listen, boys, listen. Ten or fifteen thousand dollars, gold, is a lot of money, ain't it? Well, like I was telling you when we got the signal he was coming up, Monroe has got that gold packed away somewheres. Years ago, when times was bad, he needed money, and no bank or anybody'd let him have it. Monroe swore he'd never again be caught without a pile of cash right where he could put his hands on it. He's got that money—twenty thousand he took out—and we ought to get it before—before anything happens to him."

"I think we'd better shoot him, *then* look for the money," said Perley Price.

"A fine chance we'd have to nose around the ranch out there with the Waxman boys setting on the corral, watching!"

"Kill them, too," said the cruel Wolf-face.

"How do you hope to get it?" asked Perley Price, always interested in money.

"If we get him off somewheres and poke hot splinters under his toenails, I reckon he'd tell us," Hamel suggested.

"That'd be worse'n trying to bite the head off of a rattler," said Crawley.

"I reckon things'll work out all right if we move careful," said Hamel.

"You mean *you're* going to be careful to see that things work out all right for *you*," said young Timkins.

"Why, we're all in this together, aren't we?" Hamel asked soothingly.

"Are we? I was just wondering. You pile all the blame on Perley, here, and me. You did it yourself. We've got your letter, Hamel, telling me and Perley to come into this country and clean up on the boys. You don't even protect your own friends. You pay men wages, then count on us taking them away and whacking up with you. Yeah. We may have to leave the country but when we go, we leave that letter. Ain't that right, Perley?"

The fat gambler nodded. Sweat dribbled from his forehead. He wiped his face and sat down.

"Aw now, boys, everything'll be all right," said Hamel. "You just lay low for a couple of days. Now I'm going down and watch that redhead get his neck broken on Hellbender. Leastways, I hope so."

"I don't," said Timkins, rubbing at a bump on his head. "I want to plug him."

"You know damn well, Hamel," Perley Price said, looking up thoughtfully, "that Monroe himself cleaned out those men over at the barn last night. They may have got excited and thought it was a good chance to pot him."

100

"But you heard what he said?" Hamel asked.

"Yeah," Timkins spoke up. "He said you were afraid to call him a liar."

"I'll have some grub and booze sent up to you boys. Just lay low. That's all. Lay low."

CHAPTER 10.

Old Bill Lays a Bet

Word had got about that Hellbender was to be ridden, and some of the storekeepers shut up shop. There would be very little business while that show was going on. So a crowd gathered. Men climbed up and sat on the little corral where horses were kept overnight if the blacksmith was too busy to shoe them. Others stood about, chewing tobacco, whittling, listening to the talk, now eyeing the horse, now peering toward Red.

Blackie in a loud voice was telling that he had bet three hundred dollars. Other men rattled coins in their pockets. Hellbender had never been ridden. But men were a bit shy about betting against old Bill Waxman.

Men asked Monroe which way he was betting, and Monroe coldly replied, "I ain't betting."

Men sensed that there was something a little mysterious in the air, but word got about that Monroe was merely trying out this redhead to see if he was good enough to take on the work of busting broncs for the Zee Zee. Monroe had queer notions.

One of Hamel's Cross Bar men, carrying a fair load of liquor, came up to Red and poked out twenty dollars. "That says you can't ride him, feller."

Red did not have twenty dollars. He shook his head, not answering. He did not feel happy. If they had simply saddled Hellbender and let him climb the horse without palaver and fuss, he wouldn't have felt the least nervous, but all this rigmarole was disturbing.

"Hey, he won't even bet on himself," the Cross Bar man called vaguely to the crowd. "I got twenty says he can't ride him."

Men looked expectantly toward old Bill, but he was standing near the stirrup of the half-breed Sam and seemed disinterested. As Red appeared to have no more backing, other men drew their money. Hamel, after a private word or two with the blacksmith, patted his pockets. Offers were made boastfully.

"Time to begin saddling up, ain't it?"

"What we waiting for?"

"What saddle's he using?"

"We're trying to get somebody to take our money," said a man who had joined with Hamel in offering to bet against Red.

A couple of men busily took the saddle off

Red's horse while the half-breed Sam, with beady eyes aslant, watched them.

Monroe stood gloomily alone. He was in pretty much of a dark mood, half wondering if, after all, he wasn't putting the boy to a more than needful test. After all, if this redhead did ride Hellbender, what would it prove? Nothing, except that he was a good horseman. Some of the best bronco busters in the country were not much good as men, though they had grit. No doubt about that. Riding Hellbender or ten Hellbenders would not change the color of Red's hair. Monroe's impulses swept him this way and that. One minute he was hopeful that the boy would ride it out. The next he felt that there would be satisfaction in seeing the horse kill him. That would confirm Monroe, almost super-stitiously in the feeling that, after all, this was no son of his. Monroe did not want to admit, even to himself, that he had been in the wrong. Yet more than almost anything else in the world he wanted to believe that his son had come back to him—unmistakably his son, and a man. It was a terrific emotional experience for Monroe, and his face was clouded with a look that caused people to eye him and keep away.

"Ain't nobody going to bet on that feller?" cried the drunken Cross Bar man.

"What's the odds?" a voice inquired from the top of the corral fence.

"Two to one! Yessir!"

"Make 'em ten to one," the voice answered, "and I'll take a quarter's worth!"

The blacksmith had got his hands on the saddle and was carrying it toward Hellbender.

"Hey, Bill," said Hamel, "aren't you going to take some of this two-to-one money?"

Old Bill turned slowly, drawled, "Yeah?" then looked for a moment at Red. "How much you offering?"

"Any amount!" Hamel shouted, wanting everybody to hear him.

"Yeah? Umm. Any amount, umm? Well. That the kid can't ride him? Well, I'll tell you, Hamel. I got a couple of hundred steers that run with the Zee Zee. Me and my brother. Half of 'em are mine. A hundred steers at twenty dollars a head— that'll be two thousand dollars, won't it? You're offering two to one, unh? I'll just make out a bill of sale for my steers and put it up against four thousand dollars. How's that, unh?"

Red's heart gave a couple of jumps as if it were turning somersaults, and he caught his breath.

Hamel caught his breath, too. But men had overheard Bill's offer. Hamel glanced anxiously to where the blacksmith and another man or two were spreading the blankets over the saddle that lay on the ground.

"I haven't got that much handy, Bill."

"Umm. You mean you don't want to bet?"

"I'll write an IOU against your bill of sale."

"All right. There's Judge Tiller hustling down here so he won't miss anything. He'll hold the stakes and see it's all fixed proper, unh?"

The judge was a small man in a long black coat. He knew very little about law and being a politician, was hand-in-glove with Hamel. He came bustling up, always glad of the chance to appear important.

Bill drew a worn notebook from his vest pocket, hunted for the nubbin of a pencil, squatted down, and with the notebook on his knees laboriously and with much misspelling wrote out a bill of sale. Hamel gave over an IOU.

Monroe moodily looked on, saying nothing, but his dark eyes lingered on old Bill's face.

"Good gosh almighty!" said Red in a low voice. "Why'd you do that, Mr. Waxman? I *can* ride, but hell! Better men than me's been thrown so danged far they missed a couple of meals walking back."

"Why? Why, because I want that four thousand dollars, son."

"You'll get 'em or I'll turn sheepherder."

"You wouldn't be good herding sheep. You don't look onery enough. Now you 'tend to the saddling."

For the past half hour Red had felt like a sort of puppet. Now he came to life with a hitch at his belt and a jerk at his hat brim, and with long-legged stride and jangling scrape of spurs started toward the horse. Men who hadn't found seats on the corral followed in a spreading circle, stirring the dust. Monroe, watching his chance, pulled at old Bill's arm. He spoke in a low, half angry tone.

"Why'd you do that?"

Old Bill looked up at him with steady gray eyes, not answering.

"I asked you a question, Bill."

"I heard but I was just thinking maybe you didn't want an honest answer."

"I want to know."

"You're liable to get all het up."

"Tell me."

"The boy can ride. Look at them legs. Like a pair of Injun bows."

"That's no answer."

"I know it. But y'see, I'm thinkin' of Mrs. Monroe. All these years your personal affairs haven't been any of my business. Nor now, only since you've arranged this little bucking match to convince yourself that you made a mistake years and years ago—well, I'm just betting that Mrs. Monroe was as fine a woman as ever lived."

Monroe's dark face was lit with a flash of anger. Old Bill stood awkwardly but calm, expectant, untroubled.

"Damn you!" said Monroe.

"Yeah?"

"You and your brother—" Monroe stopped. He was a bitter man, a dangerous man, hot-tempered, unreasonable, yet even in anger had the appearance of being grimly cool.

"Me and my brother?" Bill inquired in his imperturbable drawl.

Down at the bottom of his heart Monroe was an honest man; cruel, at times almost senseless, a little mad or very near to madness. But he knew the Waxmans were square men and had been his friends. For one of the few times in his life Monroe made a complete about-face. He reached out with one long arm in a quick, hurried move, fastened his hand on Bill's shoulder, jerked him closer, and in a low hoarse voice said, "If you lose that bet, I'll pay it."

CHAPTER 11.

The Riding of Hellbender

All right," said Red at the blacksmith's elbow, "you can go over there and climb a fence post."

"Just stand back, kid. We'll saddle him for you." The blacksmith flourished a big grimy palm.

"Yeah, but when it comes to saddling a horse, it's like getting married. Nobody else can do it for you—satisfactory."

Men heard and snickered. Red was standing flat-footed, with hat brim up-tilted.

"Why, I always saddle him for fellers," said Blackie.

"And he's never been ridden, either, has he?"

"See here, meaning what?" The blacksmith swelled out muscularly, glaring.

"Meaning any damn thing you want to think I mean. Nobody touches my saddle but me."

Sitting high above the huddle of men who stood about, the half-breed Sam watched, heard, and grinned. He began to think that he understood why old Bill Waxman had banked so heavily on this boy. The blacksmith looked explosive and at last said, "That's my horse."

"And it's my saddle that goes on him!"

"All right." The blacksmith pointed at the saddle on the ground. "Go to it, then."

Red eyed the saddle with elaborate concern. "That isn't mine."

"Ain't yours?" said the blacksmith sounding as if he were trying to speak and drink at the same time. "It came off your horse."

"Yeah, and if somebody's fist bounced off your nose, you'd think 'twas your own knuckles, unh?"

Men chirped and cackled. The blacksmith was the strongest man in town but he was bad-natured and a bully. He was nearly twice as big as Red and could have broken his neck with one hand. It hurt his feelings to be laughed at, but there was nothing he could do about it. It hurt his feelings even worse to learn that the saddle lying there was not Red's, but there wasn't anything he could do about that, either.

"All right, then, saddle him yourself. Go to it. Let's see you. If you get kicked so you can't ride, we win all bets. You got to saddle him all by yourself, too, or all bets are off."

"You're a cockeyed liar!" said Red. "Nothing was said about saddling. If it takes twenty men to do it, that's got nothing to do with whether or not I ride him. Do I make myself clear? Or do you want some more information—which I got plenty of!"

Hamel was twitching at the blacksmith's shirt. He whispered nervously.

Blackie spoke sullenly. "Don't worry. He couldn't ride a stuffed mule."

"Yeah, Blackie, maybe so. But he seems willing to ride *you,*" Hamel observed.

The blacksmith turned and looked up into the beady eyes of the half-breed Sam, who grinned, then swung off his horse and began to uncinch the saddle. The blacksmith and Hamel exchanged startled looks of understanding.

Hellbender was not a horse that stood with sullen patience and let himself be saddled, then awakened explosively the minute a foot went into the stirrup. He began fighting as soon as anybody got near enough to be kicked. He was a thoroughbred outlaw, a man-hater, a man-killer.

109

It took a powerful man to hold his head, an alert, quick, cautious man to cinch the saddle.

When Red got near, the horse faced about, laid back his ears, and with long outthrust of neck, snapped.

"You son of a gun!" said Red.

The horse stood close to the post to which he was tied. This was a snubbing post staked out in the open and was scarcely ever used, except for Hellbender's exhibitions. As Red had guessed, the horse was a thoroughbred, or at least of thoroughbred strain, intelligent as a man and as wicked. He had been trained by being tormented until he was a man-hater.

Red edged up slowly, cautiously, to get hold of the slipknot, and Hellbender snapped again. Red jerked back his arm. Men laughed. Taunts began to go up. The blacksmith's hoarse voice was loudest.

"Yessir," said Red to himself, growing hot as if with prickly heat, "I reckon I'd laugh, too, if I was setting on the fence, watching." He spoke aloud, soothingly. "You, Heller, you. I ain't blaming *you* none. But if all horses had your disposition, cows'd have to get along as best they could with fellers herding 'em on foot. Get away from that post."

Red jerked off his hat and slapped it at Hellbender's head. The horse, used to blows, jumped back with a high toss of his head. Red caught the end of the rope, took a quick turn about the post, and pulled. The horse sat back stubbornly, refusing to move.

"I'll hold the rope," said old Bill, coming up unhurriedly. "You go 'round back and head him this way so we can snub him up close. Get the blindfold on him. But look out, or he'll kick you higher'n a kite."

Hellbender, with neck outthrust in a stubborn pull against old Bill, regarded Red with a rolling eye.

"Move up," said Red, flourishing his hat.

Hellbender answered with a lashing hoof. Onlookers cheered the horse. They wanted to see Red have trouble. It made the entertainment more amusing.

"If I owned him," Red called to old Bill, "I'd stake him out where horse thieves was trouble-some. He'd sure make a horse thief see the error of his ways. What I need is a bull whip."

He yelped shrilly, again flourishing his hat, and the horse sidled off, but tugging against the rope, not giving an inch.

"All right, all right," said Red and went to his saddle over which the half-breed Sam stood guard.

Red took his rope from the saddle, shook it out, shaped the loop, gave it a flip behind him and a toss forward. The loop settled over Hellbender's head. At that, a few men grudgingly admitted that Red knew what he was doing. Those farthest off thought that old Bill had told him what to do; those nearer knew that Bill was saying nothing. He, as much as anybody else, wanted to see how Red would manage things.

Red walked off to one side, pulling. The horse faced him, tugging against his pull and sidling around and around. Old Bill, standing well away from the post, walked around and around, too, gently taking in the slack as the horse, pulling steadily against Red, came nearer and nearer the snubbing post.

When Hellbender found himself brought against the post, he felt tricked and began to jerk and plunge from side to side. But he was caught up short and held firmly. Yet he could still bite. With ears flat against his head he drew back his lips.

"I never knew before that the devil had four legs," said Red as he came in closer, holding an end of the rope in his right hand, ready to strike. "And I don't think I ever hit a horse on the head in my life."

Red edged nearer and nearer. He knew it would do no good but he talked to Hellbender the way he always talked to horses.

"Now listen, feller, behave yourself. We're enemies, sure, but don't be so danged disagreeable about it. I got to get a half-hitch 'round your jaw. And I'm going to burn some hide right off your nose if you ain't careful."

Hellbender snapped at him and barely missed,

but the half-hitch caught the horse around the nose, and Red, settling back on his heels, jerked. The horse went into a spasm of jerks and pawing but was held helplessly, being snubbed up close to the post with the rope bound around nostrils and jaw.

Old Bill drew the snubbing rope tighter and tied it fast, then took the other rope from Red's hands.

"Does he kick when blindfolded?" Red asked.

"He does," said old Bill calmly.

"Then I reckon I'd better borrow another rope," Red suggested.

"Sam," said old Bill, "bring that saddle and those blankets up here close, then fetch your rope."

Red took Sam's rope, shook it out, and walked around behind the horse. He held a small loop watchfully, but Hellbender kept both hind feet on the ground.

"Stir him up a little, will you?" Red called.

The half-breed struck out with his hat, and Hellbender jerked with a pounding shift of feet. Red tossed the loop with a swift underhand throw, drew it tight, and settled back on his heels. Hellbender's left leg was caught.

Men muttered commendingly. Whether or not the redhead could ride, he was good with a rope.

"You will ride him, I bet you," said Sam admiringly as he took the rope from Red's hands and swayed back.

Old Bill fastened the second rope close to the

113

post. The horse was breathing noisily, with nose half closed. It sounded as if he had the distemper.

Then old Bill took his big handkerchief from about his neck, folded it, bound it about the horse's eyes, and took a firm grip on both ears, holding the animal's head as tightly as he could.

Red shook out the blanket and laid it over the horse's back. Hellbender trembled and jerked. Red drew the blanket well up on the shoulders, adjusting it carefully. Then he picked up his saddle, laying the stirrup that would fall on the far side across the seat. He heaved it up and let it drop. Hellbender struggled wildly, but with only three legs. The half-breed Sam lay back on his pointed heels.

Red stooped with cautious reach for the front cinch, and the moment he touched it, Hellbender's right hind leg flashed up.

"Too slow, old son," said Red, fingering the latigo through the cinch ring. He drew it tight, running overlapping folds through the cinch rings, binding it carefully with a double hitch, and sticking the end of the latigo between the folds. Then he reached for the back cinch. Hellbender kicked again.

"You wall-eyed son of a loco wolf!" Red reproved him.

He pulled hard on the cinch, but Hellbender was holding what little breath he had, bulging his belly. Red kicked him hard, driving the wind out of Hellbender's belly, making him relax. A minute later Red stepped back, pushed up his hat, wiped the sweat from his face.

"I guess we're pretty near all set. Can you shake loose that rope, Sam?"

Sam shook, but the loop was drawn snug between hoof and fetlock and would not loosen.

"Hold it tight again," said Red. "Here's where I get right close to heaven and maybe get kicked inside."

He edged up to Hellbender, stooped. Then, aided by Sam's pull on the rope, he caught Hellbender's leg and, squatting, held it back and up over his knee the way a blacksmith holds a horse's leg. He loosened the noose, tossed it off, then dropped Hellbender's leg and at the same time threw himself sidelong. Hellbender's leg twitched in nervous far-reaching kicks.

"So far so good," said Red. He was no longer in the least nervous. He had forgotten the crowd, forgotten everything except that here was a mean horse to ride. He straightened his belt and with absent-minded gesture rammed his guns deep into their holsters.

"I'd leave 'em off," old Bill suggested. "May get shook out. Besides, for the next half hour I reckon you're going to be a mite too busy to think about guns."

Red loosened the holster strings that were tied above his knees, unbuckled his belts, and swung the guns toward old Bill.

"You hold 'em, Sam."

Sam took the guns, fitted the end of the belt into the buckle, and swung them over his shoulder.

Then up came the blacksmith with a big bottle sticking out of his hip pocket and a hackamore in his hands.

"Who left the gate open?" said Red, standing squarely in front of him.

"You got to ride him with this." The blacksmith held out the hackamore.

"Yeah? What's wrong with it?"

"Nothing."

"Hmm." Red sounded skeptical. He reached for the hackamore and drew it through his fingers carefully, half expecting to see that it had been cut or weakened. Though a hackamore was not much good for keeping a bucking horse from getting his head down, still it helped the rider to keep his balance. "I reckon I'll use it."

"I'll put it on," said Blackie. "Bill, you make ready to turn loose them ropes."

The hackamore was slipped on, the ropes were loosened. Red took the end of the hackamore in his hand and stood by the saddle, ready to poke a foot into the stirrup and swing on.

"I'll hold his ears, Bill," said Blackie. "You get the ropes out of the way."

The blacksmith took a big drink of whisky, then grasped Hellbender firmly with his muscular hands. The ropes were cleared. Old Bill stepped back with lift of hand, said quietly, "All right, let him buck."

Red rammed his foot into the stirrup, reached for the horn, answering, "Let 'im buck."

At the same moment, Blackie, jerking down the horse's head, bent forward, spewed a mouthful of whisky into Hellbender's ear, jerked off the blindfold, struck the horse alongside the head, and reeled back, standing clear.

Red, as he went into the air, glanced downward into the grinning face of the big blacksmith and yelled. The next moment a misty spray of whisky flew up, shaken out of the tortured, infuriated horse. Red hit the saddle with scrambling reach of right leg, wildly groping for the stirrup. But he had met the saddle on its way up as Hellbender, with head low between front legs, clacked all four feet together in a back bend. Red went up out of the saddle as if flung. A lot of daylight showed between the seat of his pants and the cantle. For a moment he looked like a rag doll being flung by a bull pup. He came down with a jolt that sent his head lower than the saddle horn but he landed squarely in the saddle with the one foot still in the stirrup.

Without pause, Hellbender wheeled, jumped and came down stiff-legged fifteen feet away. Red reeled drunkenly. Only the bump of his knee against the saddle horn kept him from toppling, and his arms were up, away up, with awkward balancing flourishes. Men muttered approval with a bubble of oaths. The redhead didn't even show the first symptoms of a leather puller. He was taking it with hands in the air, and Hellbender was sure giving it to him.

Old Bill edged with shuffling sidelong scrape of feet up against Hamel and spoke clearly, but keeping his eyes on Red. "He ain't got his foot in that stirrup yet, but I'll bet my brother's other hundred cows . . ."

Hamel didn't answer. His heavy face was pale and strained.

Hellbender, with downward thrust of head far between his front legs, heaved himself forward with a tricky drop of his left shoulder, and Red pitched forward. He could not get his right foot into that flying stirrup. It was like trying to thread a needle held by a man with St. Vitus's dance. He curved his long legs embracingly about Hellbender's body, driving the spurs deep, and held them tensely, desperately, as a falling man holds onto a cliff's edge by his fingertips.

Hellbender knew, as well as Red himself, that only one foot was in the stirrup and he did not pause in any sullen thoughtfulness about what to do next. He went into the air with bucking heaves that made a whipcracker out of Red's neck, snapping his head until he was as dizzy as a man half drunk. But Red had locked the long rowels of his spurs into the cinch, and though he still reeled like a dummy, you couldn't have slipped a fried egg between the bottom of his pants and the saddle seat. No doubt about it, he knew how to ride. Hellbender understood that as quickly as did Monroe, who stood with a gloomy stare. His dark, hard face was as tense as if he faced a pair of guns.

The boy could ride, the horse could pitch. It was a matter of grit. Hellbender had been cruelly trained never to quit. Always, somehow, he had dumped his rider. The saddle would turn or the cinch strap break. His head was on fire from the burn of whisky. He was like—he *was*—a horse gone mad. With upfling of heels he swung his head around and snapped at Red's leg, gashing the leather of his chaps. Red, with all the strength he had, pulled on the hackamore, trying to keep the horse's head turned back while with the other hand he flailed the quirt. He wanted to teach the brute that biting didn't pay.

Hellbender went into a series of stiff-legged plunges, bending his back in convulsive humps. He switched ends, spinning almost like a kitten chasing its tail, until Red was drunk with dizziness. But his muscles had been trained from childhood to the saddle, to instinctive balance and sway, to cling with grip of knee and prod of spur. His blunt rowels tore the hide of Hellbender.

Then it came—the thing that everybody who knew the horse knew would come. The trick had killed two men and crippled another. Hellbender knew one way of making any man get out of the saddle. He began with a series of short, stiff-legged jumps, wheeled, and with upward toss of head and frantic pawing of forefeet threw himself straight up and toppled backward. It was a crash that would jar the life out of any man who was caught, and Red was almost caught.

As Hellbender reared, Red struck with the quirt, trying to make him lower his head and drop forward. Most horses that topple backward do it accidentally. Hellbender came over purposely, and came quickly; he fell with the thud of a thousand pounds, splattering the dust. Red swung a leg clear of the saddle as he was falling. He landed on both feet with heels braced for a heaving jerk on the hackamore but lost his balance, stumbled, and fell. But he held to the hackamore and with a catlike scramble and jump got into the saddle as Hellbender heaved his haunches up. This time both Red's feet found the stirrups in the second's pause between the time he landed in the saddle and Hellbender went into the air. Men broke into yelps, cheering.

Some of his fury seemed to have been taken out of the horse by the fall. It had jarred him. It had not hurt the rider at all. After a few bobbing jumps he reared again as if to try it once more. Red, on the lookout now, heaved all his weight forward and beat the horse's head with the quirt. Hellbender dropped his head almost to the ground and settled down to the steadiest bit of erratic pitching that Red had ever met.

Red's nose began to bleed, and he had a pain in his side. The buster's stitch-in-your-side. It made breathing hard. Hellbender seemed to know it. He ripped off stiff-legged hops that jarred like a hundred kicks from big boots; then he would switch ends and go into the air and come down with all four feet together on a spot no bigger than a cowboy's hat. Red coughed, spitting blood. Everything was, to his eyes, just a hazy blur. His head was snapped about as if his neck were broken. "Can't last forever!" sang through his brain, but not of himself. He knew that the most powerful horse must tire. It was just a matter of sticking. Every joint in his body seemed cracked.

At last Hellbender stopped, stiff-legged, with head down sullenly, heaving powerfully. He had to get his breath. Every nerve and muscle in Red's body rejoiced at this pause, this breathing space. He wanted to fold his arms on the horn of the saddle and just die, right then and there. But he knew that while he was resting, the horse would be resting, too. It was a matter of grit as to which won out.

"No, you don't!" said Red drunkenly and he raked Hellbender from shoulders to flank and with long-armed undercut snap of quirt caught him under the belly, making him jump, making him buck.

At that, men shouted with shrill yips. Some waved their hats. Some on the top of the corral lost their balance in the excitement of standing up to cheer. Not a muscle of old Bill's face changed. He peered steadily through bright gray eyes, half hidden by wrinkles—peered now toward the horse, now toward Monroe who stood as if frozen. The half-breed Sam fairly jumped up and down. He had flung his hat away. The big blacksmith stood with knotted fists, glowering, and Hamel's face was the color of butcher's paper.

Most of the men had never seen such riding, none of them would claim they had seen better. Hellbender was tired but he had a fighting heart. Again and again he tried to bite, only to get his face cut with the quirt that raised welts and broke the skin. He bucked but without the elastic snap that had made him so hard to stay on at first. Yet it was just as hard, even harder, to stay on now because Red was tired, more than tired. It seemed that no spot on his body didn't ache.

Hellbender jumped, hopped about, stopped again. Red cursed him. The rowels brought blood, the quirt struck. Hellbender took it with sullen stubbornness. He was not quitting, but he was resting. Red knew it would not do. They would have it all to go through again. He reached forward and raked Hellbender's neck with his thumbs, and the horse went into the air as if dynamite had exploded under his feet.

Then the onlookers did go wild. That any man would take all Hellbender could give, then thumb him, set them off like a bunch of drunken Indians. They slapped old Bill's back. They poked Hamel in the ribs with elbows. They jeered Blackie. They stamped and waved their hats, howling.

Hellbender bucked in a straight line for some two hundred yards, then paused, but spurs, thumbs, and hat roused him again. He yielded to the pull of the hackamore, turned, jumped stiff-legged; then his jumps became a gallop that weakened quickly into a sluggish sullen trot. Hellbender had been ridden.

Red guided him right into the crowd and with hazy searching of blurred eyes spotted the blacksmith. Men fell back as the horse came up. They stopped yelling. They even stopped talking, almost stopped breathing. Red was covered with blood. He looked half dead. Yet there was a gleam in his eyes that meant trouble. He said, "Whoa!" pulled with the hackamore, and Hellbender stopped, dropped his head almost to the ground, and heaved as if his heart were broken.

Red swung from the saddle and staggered as he took three or four steps, then stopped before the blacksmith. What Red said was confused. His mouth was dry and his lips were bleeding, but he cursed Blackie. "Whisky . . . horse's ear . . . you dirty . . ." Red's hands groped vaguely toward his hips, reaching for guns that were not there.

When he found that he was not armed, he stepped closer with stumbling lurch and his fist went out and up in a sudden drive straight into the blacksmith's face. He didn't have strength enough left to have choked a cat, but he had anger enough to have fought a dozen men of Blackie's size and weight. Cries went up, and some men with scrambling reach snatched at the blacksmith's arm, but too late. He drove his big fist squarely into Red's face.

CHAPTER 12.

A Mighty Smart Horse

When Red came to, he stared up into the black, beady eyes of the half-breed Sam who seemed to be holding a rock ready to drop it onto Red's face. Red shut his eyes and jerked his head sidewise. Water dribbled into his face. What had seemed a rock was a sponge. Red's head was lying on the half-breed's arm.

"Gosh!" Red mumbled, struggling to sit up. "You trying to drown me?"

Other men were standing about. They spoke quietly, staring. Old Bill bent low, peering. "You all right, son?"

"No," said Red, "I'm not." Sitting up with a dazed wobble of his head, he peered, blinking. "Where's that damn Blackie?"

Two or three voices answered at once. The half-breed's was the loudest. "Dead!"

"Unh?"

"Monroe shot him," said old Bill calmly.

"Shot him?"

"And didn't miss me more'n six inches," said one of the bystanders, measuring the distance between two palms.

"Never said a word," another man put in. "Just shot."

"Yeah, and Sam, here, had his gun out and was coming, too," said a voice.

"You bet," said Sam cheerfully. "Anybody, they hit my pardner they hit me, savvy?"

"Gosh!" said Red, feeling confused. He ran his fingers gingerly over his face. "Do I look like I feel?"

"You must be feeling pretty bad, then," one of the men agreed.

"I'm just plumb freckled with sore spots all over me."

"And my cinch strap was half cut in two," said Sam.

"It was that," another man put in.

Men had examined the razor-like slanting cut on Sam's latigo, which Blackie had thought belonged to Red. The blacksmith had been willing to see a man killed in order to win his bet.

"Have a drink?" said Sam.

It was the blacksmith's bottle. Red took it, raised

it toward his mouth, paused, stared at the bottle, then flung it aside.

"Not out of the same bottle, I don't!" Then peering up at the faces above him, "I don't blame a horse for anything he can do," he said. "And that horse could do plenty. But any man as will spit whisky in a horse's ear—he needs killing."

"You bet!" said the half-breed. If Red had said that black was gray, Sam would have chirped up and made it good with a fight. Red had a double claim on the dark half-breed's affection. He was old Bill's friend and he could rope, ride, and was willing to shoot. All of which appealed to Sam's primitive sentiments.

"Hellbender, I reckon," said one of the men, "is now your horse. Nobody else'll be claiming him."

"Gosh a'mighty," said Red, "I'd sooner ride a wagon load of dynamite."

"Put a saddle on dynamite, you could ride him. Yessir!" said Sam.

"I reckon he'd come pretty near being in the saddle when it come down," one of the men suggested.

"He damn near rode Hellbender one-legged," another commented.

"Well, 'twasn't because I wanted to. I was sure reaching wide and fancy for that stirrup. I thought somebody'd stolen it. I went so high I could hear angels singing, 'Here he comes!'"

Red stood up, pulling at his clothes. They were

sopping wet. He was covered with mud and blood. Sam had plunged the blacksmith's big horse sponge into a bucket of water and squeezed.

"Where's Mr. Monroe?" Red asked.

"Him and Judge Tiller went off uptown for a little talk," said old Bill quietly.

"My gosh, but didn't Hamel look sick!" a man remarked.

"Think you're ever going to get your money, Bill?"

"I think so, mebbe," said old Bill.

Red looked toward the snubbing post. Hellbender was there. He had meekly let himself be led and tied. He was still saddled.

"Why didn't somebody unsaddle him?" Red asked.

"We were sort of busy with things happening. Besides, he kicks like hell."

"Bring up some water, somebody. He's near dying for a drink."

Red went up to the horse and Sam followed with a bucket. Hellbender lifted his head slightly and dropped his ears back. Red set the bucket down in front of him and stood by, waiting. The horse sniffed it, hesitated, seemed suspicious, then drank.

Red with slow reach, put out his hand to scratch Hellbender behind the ears. At the first touch the horse jerked up his head, startled. He perhaps had never felt a gentle touch from a man's hand.

"Listen, you Heller, you!" Red's words were

abusive, his tone gentle. "I think your hide's stuffed with dynamite and gunpowder, but—"

Again Red's hand went out to scratch the ears, and again the horse flung up his head. But he did not snap. That was a whole lot from Hellbender.

Sam started to uncinch the saddle, but the horse kicked with upward sweep of left hind leg, and Sam jumped back, swearing.

Old Bill walked up slowly but had no sooner touched the stirrup to lift it to get at the cinch than Hellbender kicked at him.

"I reckon," said old Bill, "we going to have to rope his legs."

Red stepped up near the horse's side, reached slowly for the stirrup, and pulled it. Hellbender threw back his ears and swung his head but did not kick. Red gently pitched the stirrup across the saddle seat. Hellbender's foot twitched, but he did not lift it.

"Yeah," said Red, pleased, "you know who rode you, don't you?" He patted Hellbender's shoulder, lightly. "Listen, you just go on thinking I could do it again, will you? I don't think so myself, but I want to keep it a secret from you."

Red fingered the cinch, keeping an eye on that murderous foot which rested so uneasily. Red loosened the cinch. Hellbender stood motionless. Red pulled at the saddle. No move from the horse.

"You laying for me? Want to get me when I'm not expecting it?"

He loosened the other cinch. The horse shifted nervously but did not kick. Red pulled off the saddle. The blanket came with it and fell to the ground. Hellbender jumped sidelong, startled. Then he shook himself from tail to ears.

Red put down the saddle, picked up the blanket, and tossed it behind him. The horse eyed him suspiciously. Red stepped up, with hand out. Hellbender sidled off. Red edged nearer, talking. His fingers touched the horse's neck. Hellbender flinched. Red followed, moving gently, talking. After a half dozen attempts the horse stood still as Red patted his neck. Red's fingers went up behind the ears, scratching. Hellbender showed his teeth but did not snap. Gradually Red's hand slipped down on the horse's face, rubbing at the welts. Hellbender stood sullenly submissive.

One of the bystanders started around behind the horse. Instantly both heels lashed out. The fellow staggered back, not hit but barely missed. He cussed good-naturedly as the other men laughed at him.

"Mighty smart horse," someone said. "He knows who rode him."

"Somebody bring me a brush and currycomb?" Red asked.

During the next half hour, Red went over the horse from nose tip to hind fetlocks. Hellbender flinched and sidled, put back his ears, his legs twitched, but he did not bite or kick.

"I just wonder," said Red, "if I can saddle him again."

He picked up the blanket. The horse threw back his ears with outthrust of nose and bared teeth. The blanket fell. Hellbender jumped but did not struggle. Red laid on the saddle. He drew the cinches.

Men mumbled in astonishment.

"Now if I had a bridle," Red suggested.

Sam brought his own. Red adjusted the cheek straps and held up the bridle. Hellbender set his teeth. Red cautiously poked a thumb into the horse's mouth, well back of the teeth, prying. The bit slipped in. Hellbender champed and shook his head.

"Now I'm going to take a chance," said Red.

He fastened the end of the hackamore to the saddle horn, fitted his foot into the stirrup, and swung up. Hellbender jumped and came down stiff-legged but stopped still. Red clucked, patting his neck. The horse started off in a slow, dispirited walk.

Men swore, amazed.

"You see," said Red, as he swung off, "he has been ridden before. He's bridle-wise. He's been mistreated and spoiled. Now he appears not to hold a grudge. He don't act happy a-tall but he does act willing. And that's the best quality a man or horse can have. Am I right, Mr. Waxman?"

"Son," said old Bill, grinning a little, "right now

130

my sentiments about you are such that I'd agree with 'most anything you said."

"Yeah," a man spoke up. "You put four thousand dollars in old Bill's pocket."

"'Tain't there yet," said another, mumbling skeptically.

The men who overheard the remark made no comment, but understood clearly what was meant. Hamel was tricky. He would sooner let go of his own leg than a thousand dollars. Red and Sam, being busy with Hellbender, had not heard. Old Bill, of course, had heard what the man said but did not reply with word or look.

"Now me," said Red to old Bill, "if you think maybe I'm going to have some wages coming one of these days, I'd like to buy some duds. I don't mind having my shirt washed once in a while, but I like to be outside of it at such times. Liable to get soapsuds in your eyes."

"You can buy the store and put it on your back if you want," said old Bill.

CHAPTER 13.

Red-headed and Gangling

Red, accompanied by old Bill, Sam, and another man or two, took the horses to the Stage Company barn, where Red looked about with a good deal of interest at the bullet marks men pointed at and talked about. Schmaling Mem. Pub. Library
501 Tenth Avenue
Fulton, IL 61252

On the way up the street to the General Store they met Mr. Monroe and Judge Tiller.

Monroe talked a little, in a more kindly tone than most men had heard him use, and looked at Red with an expression very close to affectionate pride, even dropping a hand on his shoulder.

But the judge eyed Red with pop-eyed interest, was loud with commendation, and hurried to offer a lighted match as Red rolled a cigarette.

"I'm going up to the hotel to talk business with a man," said Monroe. "You come along up, son, after you get some new clothes."

Out in front of the General Store was a buckboard. A man, as if old Bill did not notice everything that came within range of his eyes, pointed and said, "Some of the Morgans appear to be in town. Some of the lady folks, I reckon."

Judge Tiller, who had come along with them after leaving Monroe, said, with waggle of long black coat and pompous voice, "I will take pleasure in introducing our young friend to Martin and assuring him that the boy has plenty of credit, plenty of credit."

Old Bill, Sam, and the others then went on toward the Cross Bar Saloon, having it in mind to collect the four thousand dollars from Hamel.

Inside the store the judge made a sort of Fourth of July speech in explaining to Martin, the owner, that this boy had ridden Hellbender, had won the devoted friendship and admiration of Mr. Monroe, and that anything he wanted, "Anything, sir!" was to be charged against Mr. Monroe's account.

Judge Tiller settled back on his heels and waved a palm, quite as if ending a speech before a crowd.

At that moment a curly-headed cowboy with dark eyes and a good-natured face, who had been reading off a grocery list, edged up close and peered hard at Red's battered face.

Then the curly-head looked as if he were just about to explode with excitement, and yanking off his hat he slapped it over Red's back.

"Well," he shouted, "I'll be gosh-darned horn-swoggled and jiminy-cracked if it ain't old Red Clark of Tulluco himself! Well, you old piece of poison weed, you! Dang my hide! How's all the home folks?"

"Harry Stow!" gasped Red.

Red and his old friend, who was also from Tulluco, pumped hands, slapped each other on the back, almost embraced, gave a fair imitation of an Indian war dance, and young Stow let go of some whoops that seemed to quite paralyze the amazed judge, who rocked back on his heels with mouth open and long coat tails aflutter. The storekeeper edged away anxiously, wondering if the Stow boy had not tanked up on whisky which was just beginning to take effect.

"And it was you, was it, that rode that horse I been hearing about?" Stow shouted. "Well, if I'd got to town a mite sooner, I might've saved 'em the trouble of exercising that poor old animal by telling these here Tajola folks what I know of Red Clark and his riding abilities! Why, you can ride anything that's got a belly for a cinch to hold to. Hell's bells and the devil's whiskers, but I'm gosh-a'mighty glad to see you, Red."

"Well, since you're getting so dang personal," said Red, "I'll throw that compliment right back in your face. What you doing here?"

"Me? I'm working for the best outfit in the country. Old Oliver Morgan. I just drove in Mrs. Morgan and one of the girls this morning and am getting some grub."

Red clean forgot all about his name being, or supposed to be, "Frank Peters," and was joyful at having met a fellow he had known almost from babyhood.

A few minutes later Judge Tiller got Harry Stow out in the alley back of the General Store and asked some questions.

"How long have I known Red Clark?" said young Stow. "Why, ever since I was big enough to crawl. I used to steal the bottle out of his crib. Yessir. Me and him was twins almost."

"You knew his people?"

"Knew 'em? Knew old Sheriff Clark of Tulluco? Why, the sheriff used to spank me the same as if I was his own son. There wasn't a finer fellow ever lived than old Sheriff Clark, and his son is just like him."

Judge Tiller had much cunning and listened encouragingly. Stow gladly told all he knew about Red with enthusiasm and praise.

Then the judge with hasty trot of short legs and flap of coat tails went straight up the alley to the Cross Bar Saloon. He fidgeted nervously on the back stairs while a fellow to whom he had spoken went up front and spoke to Hamel.

Hamel was up at the bar with old Bill Waxman, who was waiting sort of patiently but firmly to be paid four thousand dollars, while the beady-eyed half-breed Sam lingered close by. Hamel was sweating and puffing. He acknowledged the debt, though with a rather hasty murmur he did try to point out that when Hellbender fell, Red had got out of the saddle. Old Bill's steady gray eyes did not flicker, but Sam's beady ones snapped. Hamel did not stress that technicality. Red had stayed in the saddle while the horse stayed on its feet, and that was riding according to the rules of the range. But Hamel pointed out the scarcity of gold. Four thousand dollars. Why, the Cross Bar Saloon itself wasn't worth four thousand dollars!

"Give me time," said Hamel.

"I gave a bill of sale on my cows," said old Bill. "If I'd lost, you'd have had your men riding out by this time to round 'em up."

"I'll pay. I'll pay, of course. But be reasonable, Bill."

It was then that a man plucked at Hamel's sleeve and whispered.

"Someone wants to see me. I'll be right back," said Hamel.

Judge Tiller was hopping on one foot, then on the other, as if he stood on a hot griddle. He reached forward, buttonholing Hamel, and whispered excitedly, "I've just detected one of the biggest swindles ever attempted in this here country, Hamel. Let's go where we can talk."

They went upstairs and into one of the unused back rooms. The floor, long unswept, was so covered with dust that their feet left much the same sort of tracks as if in light snow. The windows were grimy. The judge jerked off his broad-brimmed black hat and beat at his face, fanning himself.

"Monroe made me promise never to speak of this, Hamel, but something has come up," said the judge. He was a fidgety little man who never did anything without being advised, backed up, supported; and in nearly everything that came up he consulted with Hamel. "Monroe, sir, he thinks that red-headed boy is his own son!"

A look of amazement spread over Hamel's heavy face. He had heard clearly enough, but asked, "What? What's that? What'd you say, Judge?"

"Yessir. After that riding this morning, sir, he came to my office and made out a will leaving everything to his dear son, Jerome Douglas

Monroe. But," the judge added hastily, "you mustn't let on that I've told you."

Hamel put out a hand gropingly toward a chair. His brain felt a little blurred, but one thing he understood clearly enough; that was why Monroe had been so mysteriously angered by the attempt to kill the boy.

"But," said the judge, bending forward and half whispering, "he's no more Monroe's son than you are. There in the store just now . . ."

In less than five minutes' talk, the judge and Hamel, by putting what they thought were two and two together, came more or less sincerely and with great excitement to the conclusion that the Waxman brothers and Red Clark had rigged up a swindle on Monroe.

"And they would have succeeded but for me," said the judge, unconsciously poking out his chest and standing as if awaiting some applause.

Hamel slapped his hand down on the dusty table and gazed broodingly into space. Then, almost admiringly, "I never thought the Waxman boys had so much brains."

"Or could be such scoundrels," said the judge indignantly. The judge was not a very honest man himself but seemed so through always being indignant at rascals.

"I've got it!" said Hamel, bringing his fist down on the table as he arose. "You fetch that Stow boy here. I'll hustle up to the hotel and get Monroe. I won't let on that I know anything more than that you've sent me. Monroe and the Stow boy can talk. That'll fix them Waxmans' and that red-headed skunk."

Hamel was excited by the honest feeling that for once in his life he was exposing somebody else's trickery.

As Hamel left by the back way and hurried up to the hotel, his tricky brain buzzed. He saw a way to wriggle out of paying Bill Waxman any part of the four thousand dollars. Moreover, in a hazy sort of excitement, he vaguely saw—or thought he did—how it would be possible to steal the Waxman boys' idea for swindling Monroe. Hamel really felt a little disappointed with himself that he hadn't thought of the trick himself long ago. If Monroe died, then he, Hamel, using the judge's influence, could run in almost any young stranger as Monroe's son, sell off the Zee Zee cattle, water, and land, divide the money and get out of the country. That was something to think about.

As he went on to the hotel porch, he saw Mrs. Morgan talking with the doctor and young Margie Morgan standing by. Hamel bowed and lifted his hat, but the two women eyed him coldly.

He went in and called Monroe aside.

"Mr. Monroe, Judge Tiller is all excited," said Hamel. "He says for me to come and get you quick. He says he's just learned who that red-headed feller is. I don't know just what he means, but he says the fellow ain't a-tall who you think. He's got a man that knows who the redhead is, and is waiting for you to come and talk to him."

Monroe's face grew dark. He eyed Hamel as if angered, then pulling down the brim of his hat, said, "Come!" and started off, making Hamel trot to keep up with his long-legged stride.

On the porch he passed the Morgan women without looking toward them, and they stared after him without friendliness.

Upstairs over the Cross Bar Saloon, in the same dusty back room where Hamel and the judge had talked, the judge was now waiting with young Harry Stow.

Young Stow knew Monroe by sight and had no liking for him. He began to feel a little as if he had been trapped in this back room with these three men. The judge, friendly with all men, was more or less friendly, too, with Oliver Morgan, so Stow hadn't minded talking to him. But Hamel and Monroe were different.

"I gotta go. Mrs. Morgan'll be wanting me."

"But Mr. Monroe, here, has become very interested in your friend," said the judge smoothly. "He has hired him. He would like to know just who the boy is. He has planned to do a great deal for your friend."

"He's Red Clark of Tulluco. One of the best fellows that ever lived—and I mean it."

"You have known him a long time, I believe?" the judge inquired.

"We grew up together."

"Just what has he ever done to make you admire him so much?" said the judge coaxingly.

"He's square. He sticks. You can bank on him. Mrs. Morgan don't know where I am and she's wanting to make an early start. I'll be going."

"You say," the judge queried, "that he is the son of the sheriff of Tulluco?"

"Of Sheriff Clark, yessir."

The judge looked up intently at Monroe, whose face was tense.

"Anything you'd like to ask, Mr. Monroe?"

"Did you ever know his mother?" Monroe asked.

"She died when he was a tiny kid."

"Does he look like his father?"

"Him? Yeah. Red-headed and gangling, with the same eyes. Only the sheriff was a fellow that didn't laugh much. Red's full of fun. I gotta be going. Only I'll tell you this," said Stow, looking straight at Monroe, "you never saw a man so gosh-blamed willing to fight as Red is when he's riled, and he won't back down from the biggest man living. And he's honest—just like his old dad, the sheriff. And listen, when bank robbers or road agents got off with something and Sheriff Clark went after 'em, he'd come back with whatever it was the fellers stole. There wouldn't be no five or

140

six hundred dollars missing like when most sheriffs recover loot. I gotta be going."

He left, glad to get away from them, and walked with heavy thump of boots. He felt that he had surely spoken up for Red in a way that would help men to admire him. But he, in his loyalty to Oliver Morgan, was a little regretful that Red had thrown in with the Monroe outfit.

When Stow had gone, no one said anything for a time. Hamel turned to a window and tapped the dusty sill thoughtfully, trying to pretend that he wasn't curious. The judge, a little furtively, watched Monroe. Monroe, with hat pushed back, stared at the doorway through which young Stow had passed.

Monroe spoke coldly, without looking around, "That paper I had you make out this morning— tear it up."

"I'll do that, sir," said the judge.

Hamel glanced quickly about, meaning to catch the judge's eye. But Tiller did not notice.

"You can't trust any man, ever," said Monroe, barely aloud and bitterly.

"I'd never have suspected them Waxman boys," the judge murmured.

"There's no doubt as to what they were up to," Monroe agreed calmly. "They brought him here to fool me. Old Bill knew the boy could ride. That's why he backed him so heavy this morning. They had me fooled."

"And look at the way Buck Waxman cut and run," said the judge. "He was scared the plot had been knocked to flinders."

Monroe nodded.

"Why, what's wrong, Mr. Monroe?" Hamel inquired solicitously. At the same time he gave the judge a wink.

Monroe told him his suspicions. Hamel displayed astonishment and indignation. "I never did trust them Waxman boys, never," he remarked.

"I don't know what to do," said Monroe, dropping into a chair and staring moodily at the floor. It was unlike Monroe to say that; it was unlike him ever to hesitate.

"Do!" said Hamel, popping his eyes and puffing his cheeks in his best effort to show amazement that Monroe would not promptly get into action.

"I liked that boy. I sure did," said Monroe sullenly.

"I sure didn't," Hamel blurted.

"And the Waxmans—I always trusted them," Monroe added.

"Can't trust any man," Hamel declared. "Them Waxmans meant to kill you. Kill you and run in that redhead as your son. And—" this was oily solicitousness—"they know, don't they, where you've got your money hid?"

Monroe nodded.

Then Hamel nodded repeatedly, just as if something he suspected had been proved. He murmured huskily, "Sure are deep ones, the Waxmans."

"I think I'll have a talk, private, with old Bill," said Monroe.

"He'll lie like hell," Hamel urged. "Won't he, Judge?"

The judge was helped to answer emphatically by a nudge from Hamel's elbow. "Indeed! Most assuredly."

"I reckon there can't be any doubt," Monroe said, reluctantly though. "They must've meant to kill me and steal the ranch. And they damn near got away with it. I'll just go down and have it out with Bill. Then with that damned redhead."

"That's the talk, Mr. Monroe. Ain't it, Judge?"

The judge, not liking to be poked in the ribs by Hamel's elbow, stepped hastily to one side, but he affirmed that Monroe must attend to the matter in his usual direct manner.

At the first opportunity for a furtive whisper, Hamel said, "Don't you tear up that will, Judge. Don't do it. I've got an idea. You being administrator and all—a great idea."

CHAPTER 14.

Not Likely to Die With Boots on

R ed, finding his credit was good in the store and seeing a lot of nice things, splurged. He felt so battered, bruised, and knocked about that some gay trimmings seemed needed to set him off. He stuck a sportive broad, stamped leather band on the crown of his old hat, tied a broad red-and-yellow-silk handkerchief about his neck, got into a gay blue shirt, bought himself a pair of buckskin gloves—which he would never wear. He bought a new pair of blue pants and a pair of chaps—without fur, fringe, or bat wings, but lined down the seams with conchos. Then he got himself a new pair of almost skintight boots, and set them off with new stamped leather straps for his spurs. Red had a bit of a weakness for finery. The interested storekeeper tried to get him to take new cartridge belt and holsters, but Red balked.

"No, sir. I like to look nice and all that, but I'd rather get married blindfolded than poke my guns into strange holsters."

Red took some boxes of .45s, and his bill came to seventy-six dollars.

That seemed a lot of money for the little doodabs, but as Red said, "Fixings come high."

He peered at himself in a hand mirror, shook his head, and looked away.

"If I was in a handsome men's contest I'd sure have to wear a mask."

He had been told to meet Monroe at the hotel, and he now hurried there, but he hadn't gone far before he wished he had on his old boots. These were handsome, highly polished, but they pinched. The flap of the gloves in his belt annoyed him, so he stuck them into a hip pocket. The hatband was heavy. The silk handkerchief about his neck was light and fluttered. The spur straps didn't set quite right.

As he came up to the hotel porch he saw a pretty girl standing there, all alone. She looked at him with calm frank interest. She guessed who he was, having heard about the redhead who had ridden Hellbender. But Red got all warm inside and embarrassed. He knew he had a black eye and a bruised cheek.

By the look of her she was a range-bred girl, and all this new finery must—he thought—make him look like a fool tenderfoot in her eyes.

He had turned his back on her and was making for the barroom when he heard a shout. "Hey, Red."

Harry Stow came up at a run, overtaking him, and began talking when still some feet away.

"Say, Red, a funny thing. I'm sure your friend. Monroe, Hamel, and that Judge Tiller got hold of me and asked all about you. I told 'em that old Red Clark of Tulluco was—Why, what's the matter?"

"You sure have spilled the beans and put your— I mean *my* foot in it! I never thought to tell—I couldn't've told you. Harry, don't you ever go and do anything dishonest, 'cause us fellers that ain't got the habit are plumb sure to—Lord gosh! but I ought to've lit out with old Buck last night. I wonder where I can find him? I'd like to snuggle up in his blankets—snores and all."

Then Red heard a cool pleasant voice. "I know where Buck is. If you have a message—"

He turned and faced the girl.

"This here is Margie—I mean Miss Morgan," said young Stow with a vague proprietary air.

"You know where he is?" Red asked.

"He came over to the ranch, early this morning. That's why we came to town. About the boy that was hurt. We're taking him home with us."

"What boy?" Stow asked, surprised and not exactly delighted.

"The boy that was shot last night. Buck and Mother had a long talk. With Dad."

"Is he out to your ranch, miss?" Red inquired anxiously.

"No, but I know where to find him."

"Where?"

"I can't tell you. But if you have a message?"

"All right, you tell him I want something nice put on my tombstone. You tell him it's known all

146

over town that I'm Red Clark of Tulluco. You tell him the last you saw of me I was making tracks—long ones!—down to the barn for my horse."

"I don't understand," said the girl.

"He will. And he'd better shed plenty of tears or I'll haunt him."

At that moment the red-nosed doctor came bustling down, saw Harry Stow, and said briskly, "Mrs. Morgan says for you to bring up the buckboard. And put plenty of straw in the bed. We are ready just as soon as you get here."

The doctor went back into the hotel. Stow, with a blank look, turned inquiringly to the girl. "What's all that mean, Margie?"

"We are taking the hurt boy out to the ranch. Mother and Dad are awfully excited about him."

"Who is he?"

"I don't know. But you had better do as Mother says."

With that she ignored the poor boy who jealously worshiped her and turned to Red, asking, as young Stow went off, "Whatever is wrong?"

"Wrong?" said Red grinning. "Nothing much—only if I can't run faster'n Monroe can shoot I'm likely to get some holes in my hide. Yes'm."

The girl frowned, mystified; then asked brightly, "Are you joking? You don't appear very scared. What have you done?"

She was a pretty girl and friendly.

"Miss, I can't tell you. But maybe Buck will.

Cross my heart and hope to die if I've done anything much wrong—so far. In a way it's kind of funny. Another way, 'tain't."

"If you are a friend of Buck's you couldn't do anything really wrong."

"I'm glad to have you think so, but us men, we're terrible deceivers. Take old Buck himself. He looks so solemn and sort of timid, yet he eats fried wildcats all peppered over with tacks."

The girl laughed, then remarked earnestly, "The Waxman boys are all that has kept us Morgans from having a lot of trouble with Monroe. My dad thinks a lot of them, and so does my mother. I know Buck better than Bill and I like him. Oh, there are some men riding up, and look how they look at you."

She was a girl of the range and—in spite of some schooling in the East—had the sensitiveness of the range-born for anything that looked like trouble.

Red turned, looking toward the two men who had come up at a trot and now drew rein in the street right at the front of the hotel. He recognized one of them as Frank Sterns, a Cross Bar man who had been in the poker game when the trouble started. The other he didn't know but did not like his look. From what he had overheard the night of the shooting in the barn, Red knew that this Sterns had had a hand in the shooting of the boy through the window.

"Get back!" Red said to the girl. "Maybe there's going to be some argument."

The horsemen eyed Red. They seemed to be waiting, purposefully. With a jerk of rein and prod of spur they kept their horses sidelong to Red. He suspected that their right hands were touching guns. But they said nothing. It was as if they waited for a signal.

"Was you hombres looking for somebody of about my size and age?" Red inquired.

They eyed him steadily but did not answer.

Then Red learned what they were waiting for. The girl cried, "Look out behind!" He spun about in time to see two men come stealthily from the barroom doorway. One was a gray bleary-eyed man with a badge on his vest. "Sheriff."

Then things got mighty confused and blurred. Hamel, knowing that Red had gone up to the hotel, had sent the sheriff and some men to surround the building and get him. But Monroe had at last told that it was Red who had shot the men down at the barn. So the sheriff and men who came with him were expecting trouble.

Red saw a drawn gun in the sheriff's hand and heard him say, "Put up your hands."

Red, being an honest boy and a sheriff's son, had a lot of respect for the law. For the most part, sheriffs were to be trusted, even bleary-eyed ones. But he didn't like the look of this one nor the way he had brought so many men along with him. That seemed a sort of acknowledgment that he wasn't much good as an officer of the law. So Red hesitated just long enough for an eyelid to flicker a couple of times. The girl cried out, "Here're more, too!" and other men came from around the end of the porch.

Red was cut off in every direction. Evidently nobody expected him to put up his hands. The sheriff's order was nothing more than a signal. The two horsemen shot almost together, but Red had jumped. He flung himself back to the wall, and both guns were blazing.

There were oaths, yells, the startled crash of glass in the barroom, and the pulsing tramp of feet. Guns roared. Men dodged behind posts. Some went off the porch in such a hurry to get to a safe place that they fell as if they had been shot.

Red poured his guns at the horsemen. At the first shot, Frank Sterns threw up his hands, and the gun he held flew up as if thrown. His startled horse jumped, and Sterns toppled backward with one foot in the stirrup. That scared the horse and it bounded away, terrified by the thing it dragged.

The other horseman reeled, cursed, and with both hands pulled at reins and horn as if hanging onto his life while the horse with startled stiff-legged sidling edged across the street and stood still. Then the man slid off slowly, head first, and lay as if sleeping in the dust at his horse's feet.

Red was caught on the porch between two

groups of men, two on one side and three on the other. All in all they had brought seven men to get him. Still, while he was between two fires and the air was filled with bullets, that gave him a sort of advantage because he was hard to hit. Such bullets as missed him went by and sang into the ears of other men who were shooting at him.

Loud voices bawled confused orders. Red did not know how many there were after him. He got a blurred glimpse of the Morgan girl pressed tightly up against a post, and her mouth was open as if she were calling something, but he didn't hear what she said.

Whenever guns started to go off, Red had a way of keeping busy, and he shot fast, banging away to the right and left and knocking splinters into the faces of men who had ducked off the porch and ventured to peer over. The noise of the guns sounded as if a lot of men were in action, and all up and down the street people who had heard the shooting began to appear. Red thought they, too, were coming after him; and it surely looked bad.

His hat, with heavy band and all, was shot away. His new shirt was ripped right across the breast, and the right heel of his new boots had either been shot off or knocked off in a knot hole so that he had the swaying limp of a cripple. There wasn't a horse handy or he would have tried to hit a saddle and go. He had tried to keep count of his shots, for he had been trained to think that was about as important as shooting straight; but in the con-fusion of banging away, now to the right, now to the left, and trying to answer every shot that came at him, he had lost track, and his hammers snapped on empty shells.

That surely looked like the end. Men, taking good care to protect themselves, crouched at the end of the house and below the porch. Some of them had bullet holes in arms and legs, and the Cross Bar puncher who had jeered at Red just before the riding of Hellbender now lay all spraddled out, dead.

Red did the only thing there was to do. He wouldn't surrender and he couldn't run; at least not far. He left the wall, took three long jumps, and whirled inside the hotel doorway, scattering the startled occupants with the threat of his guns, and went up the stairs. Halfway up he met the red-nosed doctor who, at the sight of Red's guns, yelled as if the devil had come to claim him and started back up the stairs. The doctor was a bit fat, but he went like an antelope, except that he let out yells such as no antelope ever made.

Mrs. Morgan had come down the hall to see what all this shooting was about. She lived in dread of the range war that seemed always about to break out between Monroe and the Morgans. The doctor, sprinting madly, almost knocked her over. She thought at first that Red was chasing him. Mrs. Morgan was a brave woman. She also knew that no puncher would harm a woman. She put herself directly in front of Red, stopping him.

"What's the matter. What's happened? Why are you after him?"

"After who?"

"The doctor."

"I don't want no doctor—yet. You're Mrs. Morgan, aren't you? There's a lot I'd like to tell you, but I ain't got time. Monroe—Hamel—the sheriff—I've messed their men up some. Tell Buck our little show is all busted up, and—"

"You are the Clark boy from Tulluco."

"Yes'm." Red was prodding at empty shells. "And I'm going to get a room and make a stand. They're awful poor shots. Hasty-like and they shut their eyes when they pull the trigger."

"Oh!" said Mrs. Morgan thoughtfully. Then with shove and push, "Into this room here. And under the bed. Quick!"

"Me crawl under a bed?"

"Quick, I'll help you. I know all about you. There's no other way."

"But under a bed!"

She half pulled him into the room, his own room. The boy, Jerome Douglas, lay feverish and unconscious on the bed.

"Quick!" said Mrs. Morgan. "I hear them coming. Get under the bed. You'll be all right."

"Under a sick man's bed? I can't."

"Don't be a fool just because you're brave. Listen to me. This boy's mother and me—" she swept her hand at the unconscious form on the bed—"were friends. I'd do anything for him, or to spite old Monroe. Get under the bed. Buck's going to need you."

Red got down on his belly and started to crawl. It was dusty under that bed; hadn't been swept for weeks. The dust got into his nose, and he had to pinch it hard. It got into his throat, and he swallowed fast to keep from choking.

Mrs. Morgan had stepped just out of the door into the hall and was scolding. "You men have no feelings a-tall! A boy up here dying, and you— What's all this shooting about?"

"We're after that desperado, Mrs. Morgan." It was the bleary-eyed sheriff speaking. "He killed some of my men and came this way. Right up the stairs and—"

"I *did* hear somebody running through the hall. You look careful, maybe you can find him. I'm going to take this boy, here, that was shot last night out to the ranch and cure him. I'll want some help pretty soon in carrying him down to the buckboard on the mattress."

"All right, Mrs. Morgan. You just holler when you're ready and we'll help you. But now where could that feller have gone?"

"Into one of these rooms maybe," said Mrs.

154

Morgan. "That hall window is up back there. Maybe he jumped out."

Mrs. Morgan stepped back into the room and with the door half shut peered out at the men who with much hesitation had begun to open doors. They would open a door, jump back, and say, "Come on out! We've got you!" If there was no answer, they would peer in, look behind the door, under the bed and in the corners, then go to the next room.

A crowd had followed up into the hall but hung well back, not wanting to be near when the shooting started. They knew that Red would shoot.

Margie Morgan came up with hair in a tangle and eyes bright. "Oh, Mama, you ought to have seen him! That old sheriff is scared right now that he'll find him."

Just then at the end room of the hall there was a commotion, and voices shouted, "They've got him!" People surged forward, then somebody laughed. It was not Red, but the red-nosed doctor. He was trying to tell them that Red had chased him down the hall. Believing just that, he persuaded others that it was true. The sheriff then peered through the open window at the end of the hall.

He decided that Red must have jumped out of the window and would be hiding in one of the buildings out back.

"I'll stay here and keep a watch out for him,"

said the sheriff, posting himself at the window.

"Yeah, it's safer," somebody called.

The sheriff pretended not to hear.

It was then that everybody was excited by the news that there had just been a shooting scrape in the Cross Bar Saloon, and a good many people rushed down there.

Monroe had accused old Bill Waxman, his foreman, of trying to run in an impostor as his, Monroe's, son. Old Bill had simply stood wide-mouthed and motionless, not in the least knowing what it was all about. He hadn't even made a move when Monroe reached for a gun. But the half-breed Sam had not hesitated. He drew and shot Monroe, striking him in the hip, putting him down. In all the shooting scrapes that he had been in, that was the first time Monroe had ever been hit. In falling, he shot and killed the half-breed. Then old Bill, with empty hands, had walked right up to where Monroe lay on an elbow with gun leveled, and had said, "You can kill me if you want, but anybody that has been telling you I've played any tricks is a liar."

Something about old Bill, his downright honesty, the honesty of all the years that Monroe had known him, was impressive. Monroe did not shoot, though Hamel standing well to one side, drew his gun and would have fired had some-body not caught his hand.

Then Monroe said, "You men take care of Bill

and see that he don't get away. When we catch that Red, we'll get the truth out of him. Out of both him and Bill."

Then Bill said, "Nobody don't need to hold me. I'll stay right here as long as anybody wants to see me."

But they took away Bill's gun and held him as a prisoner.

CHAPTER 15.

A Handsome Buckaroo

The red-nosed doctor was hurried off down to the Cross Bar Saloon to take care of Mr. Monroe.

Mrs. Wyman was harshly indignant at the commotion that the sheriff and his men had made in her hotel. She told the sheriff in good round, loud tones that he was going to have to pay for the damage done to her windows. Some of them in the front of the house had been shot out.

The sheriff said that he allowed Red had busted as many of her windows as anybody. She came back at him in a louder tone than ever to say, "Nothing of the kind. It appears, from the number of men that have got holes in 'em, that boy didn't waste no bullets breaking windows. And if you hadn't hid yourself like a turtle in its shell, I reckon your old hide would be punctured, too.

Like now, you say you're going to stay up here and look out of the window while the other men nose about to find him. And me, if you want to know how I feel, I hope nobody finds him. I think he's a lot honester than the men that are looking for him. So there!"

The sheriff looked uncomfortable, got red as if suddenly sunburned, told a man by him that women were like a lot of cackling old hens, and allowed that Red couldn't have gone far because he had been hit as everybody could see by the way he limped.

Then the sheriff and other people began to go downstairs.

Mrs. Wyman stopped to express her feelings to Mrs. Morgan, and Mrs. Morgan pulled her by the arm into the room, saying, "Come in here." To Margie, Mrs. Morgan said, "You watch here at the door," then she closed it.

"Mrs. Wyman," she said, "I need your help."

Then Mrs. Morgan stooped down and looked under the bed.

"How do you feel?" she asked.

"I want to sneeze," said Red.

"Good gracious!" said Mrs. Wyman, hastily dropping to her knees. "Why, that's him!"

"Yes," said Mrs. Morgan. "I heard how you talked to the sheriff."

Red poked out his head and looked at the two women. Then he sneezed, rubbed his face with a dusty hand, sighed deeply, and said, "I reckon I ought to be thankful to you ladies, but it's awful hot under here, and dusty. Besides, I've got my guns reloaded now."

Margie, hearing a man's voice, opened the door and peered in. At first she was astonished, then she laughed because Red did look funny with his head out from under the bed and his bruised face streaked with dust.

"Oh, Mama, what are you going to do with him?"

"Take him home with us," said Mrs. Morgan. "I've thought it all out. He can lay down there on the mattress beside this boy, and we will cover him with blankets and have the mattress carried to the buckboard and—"

Red was coming out from under the bed with hasty scrambling. He stood up, shook himself, stamped on his heelless boot, and backed into a corner.

"Not me! No'm. I don't hide in a hurt man's bed. No'm, I'm 'shamed enough at hiding under the bed. I don't know what I'm going to do, but I won't do that. No, sir-ee! No, ma'am, I mean!"

Mrs. Morgan, who was a forceful woman and used to having her own way, tried to argue. Margie coaxed. Mrs. Wyman pointed out that it would be best. But Red backed farther into a corner and shook his head stubbornly.

"Then what are you going to do?" asked Mrs. Morgan.

"I don't know exactly but I got a notion that I'd like to plaster Hamel's hide on my saddle, the same as you do a rattler's. For an ornament!"

"They'll kill you," said Margie.

"No'm. They're poor shots. And folks that are skinny and can run fast, like me, aren't easy hit."

"I can keep you here in my hotel for a time," said Mrs. Wyman thoughtfully.

"I'd sure like to stay somewhere where it's quiet and peaceable till after dark," said Red.

"Well, if you won't, you won't," said Mrs. Morgan. "I was going to take you out to where Buck is."

"You can have Buck come to town. Tell him everything is known except that me and him is honest. If we have to bury half the town, we've got to persuade folks of that. Yes'm."

After some more talk, in which Red still stubbornly refused to fall in with Mrs. Morgan's plan, Mrs. Wyman made sure that the hall was clear and led him to a room.

"Now if there's anything you want?" she said.

"I want to rest and meditate."

Closing the door and putting a chair against it, he then peered at himself in a small cracked mirror.

"You're a fine-looking specimen of a handsome cowpuncher, you are," he remarked. "You got a black eye, a busted cheek, and your nose ain't on straight. You're smeared up like an Injun in war paint. The Morgans are nice folks, but Mrs. Morgan has got funny notions. But I never liked working on a ranch where there was women folks. They take your mind off cows. My gosh, but I'm tired! And sore. I don't feel happy. If Harry Stow marries that Morgan girl I hope she makes him unhappy. Well, it wasn't his fault I was wearing another feller's name. After this I'll stick to my own. I don't think I like this Tajola country much. But I can't get out till I've made folks understand that I'm an honest boy who just had some bad luck."

Red took off his shirt and boots, hung the guns on a bedpost within easy reach, poured water into the washbowl, and scrubbed himself with much spluttering. His face *was* sore.

Towel in hand, he paused, listening. There was some sort of commotion in the hall again. He quickly dried his hands and reached for his guns. Stooping, he peered from a corner of the window and saw the Morgan buckboard out there, with Harry Stow holding the reins and men lifting a mattress onto the bed of straw. Mrs. Morgan and the Morgan girl were busily directing the men who were doing the lifting.

At that Red felt some little assurance that men had not returned to the hotel to look for him. The Morgans would have been more interested in what was going on; they would have been listening expectantly for shots.

161

Red went close to the door and listened. He could hear the tramp of feet, a kind of low hubbub of voices, and Mrs. Wyman's voice above the others. But they stayed up near the other end of the hall. Red opened his door to the thinnest possible crack and peeked.

Monroe had been shot in the hip, badly crippled, and he was being brought into the hotel to be cared for.

Red closed the door and blocked it again with the chair. He was weary, bruised, dead tired, worn out. He adjusted one gun so that the holster was low at the side of the bed, then he took the other to bed with him. He lay down, sighed, tossed about restlessly for a few minutes, but presently curled up and slept.

CHAPTER 16.

A Jail Delivery

Red awoke in darkness and stared at the ceiling, blinking hazily. He had had the devil of a bad dream in which a bucking horse had worn six-guns on all four feet and shot at him. Then he began to piece the day's happenings together and to remember clearly enough where he was and why he was there.

He felt tenderly of his face and found it sore. He moved and his legs ached. His stomach felt empty.

"No wonder I feel bad. I haven't eaten lately. I could eat some bear cubs while their ma set by and wept, I'm that hard-hearted when I'm hungry. I wonder what time of day or night it is?"

He stirred in the bed and sat up. "I feel so sorry for myself I'd like to groan," he mused, rubbing at the joints of his knees and hips. "My face hurts me. I bet it's so black and blue I don't need to wear no mask to fool folks as to who I am. I don't dare light a lamp 'cause this window ain't got a blind."

He peered from the window into the clear starlight and listened. There was no one in sight and no sound. He drank lukewarm water from the pitcher, poured what was left into the bowl, and washed. Then he began to dress.

"If I had some whiskers, I'd sure be an old man," he said to himself, feeling rheumatic and stiff.

He began to put on his boots, but his feet were swollen. The boots were tight. He ran his fingers down to where the heel was missing. "If I had a skillet I'd fry 'em. I hear tell as how starving men eat their boots. I guess I'll go in my sock feet— and maybe step on some glass."

He buckled his guns, then drew them, working them up and down in the holsters, making sure they came easily and free.

As he drew the chair away from the door he saw something white on the floor. He picked up a piece of folded paper and moved near the window. The starlight was not strong enough for him to read by. He got down into a corner and scratched a match. A scrawling hand that wrote with a pencil had scratched:

"Folks think you got away so you are safe long as you want to stay. Old Monroe he has offered one thousan dolars for enybody as catches you. I hope nobody gets it. Mrs. Wyman."

"I sure got hopes just like yours," said Red as he tore the note to bits and stuffed them into his pocket. As he poked them deep he thought, "This letter ain't going to fall out and get somebody into trouble. That's the only nice part about making mistakes. You learn things. Me, I ought to be plumb chuck full of wisdom by this time. I must be smart to make so many mistakes and still stay alive. Most folks don't. But I won't be staying alive much longer if I don't hunt the kitchen."

He stepped on furtive tiptoes into the dark hall. Only one stairway was in the hotel, and that down to the front of the house. There was the squeak of boards under his feet, and in the stillness this sounded as loud as if tiny voices were trying to call out and tell that he was there.

"If I was a sneak thief," said Red to himself, "I'd rob only houses as had 'dobe floors." He held his breath, trying to make himself light. "I'm liable to get mistaken for a sneak thief, too, going round this way in my sock feet."

Under a door near the front he saw a light. Before he got close he could hear a querulous voice. He forgot all about food and crept near, listening.

It was a woman's voice, sharp and shrill, though not loud. Mrs. Wyman's voice. Red put an ear up almost against the door.

". . . you being bad hurt, Mr. Monroe, means you can't help yourself. Folks have always been afraid to speak up and tell you things, but now—"

"Shut up," Monroe growled in a voice of pain.

"Maybe you'd better take some more of this medicine. The doctor said it mightn't be strong enough to make you sleep, but 'twould sort of ease the pain—"

"Give it to me and get out," Monroe ordered.

There was the tinkle of glass and spoon, but Mrs. Wyman went on talking.

"It's a woman's place always to nurse sick folks. That's why I ran them men out and stayed. If I ain't never liked you very much, still even the Morgans say you—"

"Damn the Morgans!"

"—they say you're honest at heart, and I know them Waxman boys is honest, so I figure—"

"Will you shut up!"

"No, I won't. Here, you drink this and maybe you'll feel better. It's 'most one o'clock now. And it's a shame, a powerful shame, for old Bill Waxman to be in the lock-up same as if he was a drunk Mexican. The las' thing Mrs. Morgan said to me, she said, 'It's Monroe's way to mistreat folks who try to do the most for him, so I ain't going to let him know anything that I know.' And she said, just like I say, too, that them Waxman boys wouldn't know how to do anything wrong. And that Red Clark boy is just as nice a boy as ever you'd want to find."

Monroe shouted almost wildly. "He's killed a half dozen men right here in town in twenty-four hours. Nice boy! You damn women—"

"And some more of the same kind could be spared plenty without decent folks shedding a tear!"

"The Waxmans brought him here to make me think he was my son. To cheat me. Maybe to kill me and get my ranch."

"If the Waxmans did that, then I bet he is your son. Though I don't believe it, because he doesn't look a bit like you and—"

"Get out! Leave me alone! Leave me be! Get out of here, or I'll climb right out of bed and crawl downstairs into the street. Get out, will you?"

"Well, if you're going to get all riled up just because somebody is telling you things for your own good! Here's your medicine and water. You can help yourself . . ."

Red slipped off down the hall and waited near

166

the top of the stairs. He grinned, a little pleased, at having heard Monroe tormented by a spunky woman. Monroe did not like women, anyhow.

Mrs. Wyman left the room, closing the door with a bang. When she came to where Red was half concealed in the shadows, she gasped and almost threw up her hands in fright but did not make any noise.

"Oh, you," she whispered, relieved. "What are you doing out here?"

"I'm starving. Yes'm."

"You come on down to the kitchen. Follow me. I'll make sure there's nobody up."

Red followed cautiously. In the kitchen, before she lighted a lamp, Mrs. Wyman opened the door of the room where the cook slept—when the hotel had a cook—and said, "You go in there and set. Somebody might be passing and look in."

Red went into the little room, the door was left open, and Mrs. Wyman lighted the lamp, then talked to him through the doorway as she stirred busily, getting together something to eat.

"Now I want you to tell me the downright truth," she said. "Will you?"

"Yes'm," said Red, and he told the story, full and complete, to the woman, who forgot all about getting food as she stood in the doorway listening, amazed.

"Then Mrs. Morgan knows who that boy is she took home with her?"

"No doubt about it."

"You know what you ought to do? You ought to go right up to Monroe now and tell him. Or I'll do it."

"Don't do it, ma'am. Listen. As soon as ever I get me something to eat—"

Mrs. Wyman jumped, startled, as if reminded of a forgotten duty.

"—then I'll go down to the lock-up and if there's somebody down there with the key, I'll get old Bill out. If there ain't, maybe I'll do it anyhow. Least have a talk with him—"

Red stopped with mouth half opened, staring at nothing. Then he swore slowly. "I'll be gosh-danged damned! You know, I just thought of something. Old Bill, he actually believes that I'm Mr. Monroe's son. I bet you anything he does. Maybe when he finds out I'm not, he'll poke some holes into me with his gun. I wouldn't blame him much, but I don't want any holes in my hide—not even if they're made by a man I like a heap."

Mrs. Wyman would have stirred up a fire, but Red said anything that was chewable would be fine, whether hot or frozen. So she got some of the cold steaks that were being saved for hash, some cold boiled potatoes that were going into the same hash, some raw onions and a lot of catsup. His plate was heaping when she brought it to him. He sat on a chair near the dim light of the open doorway, and while she talked he ate. He said that nothing he could remember in a long while had tasted so good. He washed it down with black cold coffee, well sweetened, and said now if he had some boots, he would be a new man.

Mrs. Wyman poked about in a closet and brought out some old boots that had been left by a miner. Red stepped into them and said he could hear his toes hollering that they were lost; besides, the boots were heavy. "And who knows, Ma, but I may want to run some?" He meditated, then decided that he would have to go forth in his sock feet.

She gave him directions for finding the jail, and he set out.

The hotel bar closed at midnight, but up the street the lights of the Cross Bar Saloon were burning.

Red avoided the main part of town. It wasn't hard to avoid, there being so little of it. He crept along through the shadows and up against the sides of buildings, going cautiously and well aware that his life wouldn't be worth a bent pin if anybody recognized him—from behind.

"I must be getting easy to scare," Red mused after he had whirled about and peered toward a cat that had jumped softly from a barrel to the ground. "I've always been taught that a nice honest conscience would keep a feller strutting with his shoulders up. I sure wouldn't be no good a-tall if I felt like I'd done something that made me deserve getting shot—and Monroe's pretty

169

near right, even if he is clear teetotal wrong, in thinking I been impostoring with what law sharps call malice aforethought. From now on, henceforth forever and all time, I'm never going to use anybody's name but my own."

The jail was a squat little 'dobe building set off to one side of the town so that the drunken exuberance of such as were pitched into it would not annoy the folks who could carry their liquor without making a fuss.

Red knew all about cowtown calabooses, his father having been sheriff of Tulluco. Also, he himself had been deposited in a few and had helped get friends out of many.

"I got a notion as how there'll be somebody setting down here keeping watch over old Bill. So maybe I'd better go crawling 'round slow and expectant."

He hovered motionless and stared at the blot of shadow the little adobe building made in the starlight, but he saw no one move. That did not mean that no one was there, sitting back to the wall, perhaps half asleep or, maybe, wide awake and watchful.

Red decided to take a wide circling course and work up from behind, and so edged off, crouching low. He had not gone far through the sand before he cursed noiselessly, but with feeling, and sat down to find the cactus thorn that had stuck into a foot.

"I've heard about folks that didn't have sense

enough to come in out of the rain, but they're smart hombres to the feller that don't wear boots in a cactus patch."

He had stepped on a piece of dried cactus skin, and when he pulled it off, a piece of the thorn remained. "Now if I can find some nice broken bottles to dance on, I'll be in a plumb suitable humor to talk earnest to anybody I find hanging around this calaboose."

He went on, not finding broken bottles but plenty of sand burrs. He scratched at the soles of his feet as a dog scratches at fleas, and made such mental comments as a dog seems to make when it flops down and hastily begins to rake its neck with a hind foot.

As he came up behind the jail, he heard a queer sound, a sort of gasp and groan, then silence. He listened a long time, then decided that maybe it was some drunken man having a bad dream. Then when he got up close, he could hear a kind of gasping breathing. Somehow that didn't sound like a drunken man, and he couldn't picture old Bill making such sounds. Red was tempted to call out in a low voice but decided that he had better make sure that nobody was on guard, so he edged along to the corner of the calaboose. There, sure enough, was the blob of a shadow in a chair that was tilted back against the wall, and the man resting there held a sawed-off shotgun in the crook of his left arm.

Red's opinion of anyone who carried a shotgun was about the same as his opinion of anyone who cheated at cards.

"Hands up!" said Red, and he spoke with meaning.

The guard went into the air about the same way a jack rabbit does when it is shot and came down with hands up. The shotgun fell into the sand at his feet. "Aw, don't shoot," he begged with a kind of whiny gasp.

"Well, of all the nice folks in the world, to think I've got the pleasure of meeting you once more," said Red, stepping forward with gun hip low and leveled straight at Shorty Crawley, the barfly and stable roustabout who had brought him the false message the night before.

Shorty rose on his tiptoes so as to get his hands higher and whined, "Don't shoot! I'll tell you everything. I couldn't help myself. Don't shoot!"

"Nope, I won't. I've never shot a louse, yet. I just step on 'em or crack 'em between my thumbnails. Insulting a man like old Bill by having a thing like you guarding him! Is he in there?"

"Aw, they 'most killed him, and I begged 'em not to. They wanted to make him tell where old Monroe keeps his money hid. And he wouldn't, so—"

"All right, go on. I'm listening with both ears, but my thumb's getting tired of holding this hammer back. So you'd better talk fast—and truthful!"

172

"So they—they—his feet—tied him—and his feet—I couldn't watch. Hamel and them gamblers!"

"So that's it," said Red.

"Aw, don't shoot!"

"I'd tie you up in a gunny sack with a rattle-snake, only I'm afraid the snake would get sick after the first bite. You got the key?"

"Them gamblers've got it. The sheriff give it to Hamel and he give it to them gamblers. They've gone back to the saloon to talk over what to do next 'cause old Bill wouldn't talk. They say they're going to have to take him out and kill him somewheres so he can't tell folks what they done to him. But they think maybe he'll talk afore morning. They left me here in case somebody come down wantin' to talk to him. But I never seen you come."

Red shoved Crawley over near a barred window and called, "Mr. Waxman?"

"That you, son?" said a weak, weary voice. "I thought maybe it was you."

"I come down to get you out."

"I can't walk. What did Monroe mean by saying me and my brother tried to cheat him? Them fellers told me Monroe was dead. I'm sure sorry."

"Dead, hell! He's just got some hip bones busted. Maybe they thought you'd give in a little sooner if they told you he was dead."

"They told me, too, that you'd been bad hit."

"Me? Huh, I don't know why they'd say that when so far none of 'em has even had a chance to poke me in the *back* with a bullet. You're coming out of there, somehow."

"My feet are all burnt and my hands are tied, son."

"You won't have to do any walking." Then to Crawley, "Come around here, you. Let's see what kind of lock they got on this door."

Red picked up the shotgun, shook the sand out of the barrel, and jabbed it up against Crawley's back. He made Crawley stand facing the wall with hands up while he examined the lock. Just a padlock, but a big one. He broke the shotgun, took out the shell, then pried with the gun barrel. The barrel bent, but the lock or the staple did not give. Red threw the shotgun away.

"Well, Crawley, it's your pants or mine. So start getting out of yours. I don't like to take my clothes off in front of strangers. You hear me? Start shedding!"

"Wh-a-at?" Crawley gasped.

"I'd take 'em off your dead body—with pleasure—only somebody has to help me carry Bill. If you think I don't mean business, you just hesitate another half minute—and I'll carry Bill all by myself."

"You really mean—"

Red swung back a revolver, and without any doubt its barrel would have come down on

Crawley's head if he hadn't expressed his willingness and begun unbuckling his belt.

"Usually," said Red, critically watching Crawley take off his overalls, "when I get folks out of jail, I make 'em poke out their own pants to me. But with Bill in there the situation is some different. Now I wonder would them boots of yours fit me? Take 'em off."

"I'll get my feet all full of stickers," Crawley protested.

"You bet you will," Red agreed heartily.

Red lifted a boot, eyed it, then decided he didn't want to wear it.

"You can have your boots, but I sure want your pants."

He took up Crawley's overalls and began to fold them over the revolver, then held the gun almost against the lock and refolded the overalls. "Being a sheriff's son," said Red, "you learn a lot of things you oughtn't to do. But they come in mighty handy sometimes."

He shot. The sound was blurred, partly muffled. At least, there was no clear sharp report. Red tried the lock. The dogs had been jarred loose. He threw the overalls on the ground toward Crawley.

"If you want to wear 'em, hop into 'em lively," he said as he took off the lock and tossed it into the sand, then pushed open the door. "Come along in here, you."

"I ain't got my pants on."

"Come as you are, feller. And—" as Crawley with one leg in his overalls, the other not in, reached for his boots—"never mind them boots. I'm not wearing any. Do you good to get your feet tickled with some stickers."

Inside the jail, Red struck a match and looked down at old Bill, who sat up against the wall with his hands tied behind him. His feet were bare, raw, blistered. All about lay burned matches and a piece of candle. He stared up in silence, and his old gray eyes had fire in them, but he spoke quietly.

"They tell me you ain't Monroe's son a-tall."

"I ain't. I never meant to pretend to be. His son's the boy that got shot in the back through my window. He'd had a letter saying he was to come down here and give out that his name was Frank Peters. After he got hit by a bullet that was meant for me, I sort of took the name Peters to see what'd happen. And she's sure been happening. A lot more's going to happen, too. Damn pronto. I'm going to get you up to the hotel, then I'm going in and have a little talk, personal, with Monroe. Then I'm going down and break in the General Store, get me some guns and shells—and—and get my old boots back. After which I'm going to set fire to the Cross Bar Saloon and take 'em as they come. If you want, I'll set you in a rocking chair across the street out front, and I'll go around the back. That way we'll catch 'em front and back."

"They burned my fingers, too," said Bill.

"They'll be frying in hell, come sunup! They're coming back here to try it again, then take you out and kill you, and hide your body and pretend you got away."

Red, not at all forgetting to keep Crawley under his eye, carefully cut the thongs on old Bill's wrists.

"Now then, Crawley, much as I hate to touch you with anything but a bull whip, you and me has got to make a pack seat. Give me your hands. If you make a wiggle, just because I'm not holding a gun ready, I'll make you bite your own ears off."

Crawley was anxious to please. He held out his hands. Red arranged their hands to form a seat. Crouching, they put their hands under Bill's legs, and he put his arms about their necks and squirmed. Then they lifted him—easily, for Bill was a rather tall but not very heavy man.

It was not easy walking, but what must be done must be done. They slipped in the sand, Crawley whimpering at getting stuck by sand burrs. "You drop him and I'll kill you!" said Red and meant it. Old Bill said nothing. They went on, with Red and old Bill keeping a sharp lookout for persons who might be stirring and curious. Their hands and wrists grew weary, but Crawley was afraid to complain, and Red wouldn't. At last they came to the same barrel from which the cat had jumped and startled Red on his way to the jail. Then he said, "If you don't mind, Bill, we'll set you down here a minute." So they paused to rest, then went on to the hotel, coming up to the back door. No light was burning, Mrs. Wyman having finally gone to bed, but the door was not locked. Doors were seldom locked in Tajola.

They pushed open the door and with shuffling, struggling steps moved into the darkness. Red bumped against something. It was the stove.

"We'll set you down by it, Bill."

"All right, son."

Red laid his hand on the back of Crawley's neck, holding him, to make sure he wouldn't bolt, then struck a match. He told Crawley to lift off the lamp chimney. When the lamp was burning, Red set about tying Crawley up. He did it with twisted dish towels, drawing the knots hard. Then he dragged him by the collar into the little room where the hotel cook had slept. The floor was of pine and splintered. Crawley ventured a protest.

"Shut up," Red told him. "You stood by and watched 'em burn Bill. What right has a man got that's going to get hung to care about some splinters in his setting place? They won't bother you none with a rope round your neck."

At that Crawley began to beg and whimper, to say that he could and would tell about Hamel if only his life were spared so that he could leave the country.

"Huh," Red said, "what would a smart feller like Hamel let you learn about his goings on!"

"I've listened and overheard him and fellers talk."

"All right, talk fast and be interesting, or you'll be swung to the nearest sycamore, come sunup. And she ain't far away. Talk loud, too, so Bill in there can hear."

"Listen," Crawley gasped, "I'll tell you. They're going to kill Monroe and bring in somebody to play he's Monroe's son and get the ranch. They say they got that idea from you, and Judge Tiller is helpin'. Or they say he will help," Crawley corrected in an effort to be strictly truthful.

"Can you hear, Bill?"

"Yeah, I can."

"All right," said Red, leaning in the doorway and looking down at the terrified Crawley, "keep your tongue wagging. I ain't got much time to listen."

"They're meaning to kill Monroe and make folks think Bill got out of the lock-up and done it and lit out. Then they're going to bring in some feller to pretend to be—"

"Don't repeat yourself," Red interrupted. "We heard that before. Tell something new. What else do you know?"

"Hamel had them two detectives killed 'cause he was scairt they'd find out that him and his Cross Bar men been stealing cows from Monroe.

179

Hamel's been meaning a long time to kill Monroe but he's been scairt and—"

"Oh, shucks!" said Red. "You're just telling us now what you think will help keep your neck out of the rope. Hamel's an awful fool—any man is who don't do right—but he ain't a big enough fool to kill the only friend he's got. You stick to facts or I'll poke a gag down your throat. A wet dishrag. They make fine gags."

"S'help me God that is the truth. Ain't I been upstairs at the Cross Bar all day and most of two nights with those gamblers? Ain't I heard them talk and Hamel talking to 'em? He calculated to make me light out of town last night when it got dark on account of you guessing I come with a phony message, and Monroe, he was mighty peeved. But after he turned on you, and then after he got shot, Hamel kept me here in town. He's been wanting Monroe put out of the way because he's scairt Monroe'll learn about him stealing cattle from the Zee Zee. Them two detectives had him bad scairt and—"

Bill called from where he was sitting, "Just a minute, there. Nobody knew about them detectives but me and Monroe. I never told and he didn't. So how'd Hamel learn, unh?"

"Why," Crawley answered, raising his voice, "he reads most of Monroe's mail. Gets it from the clerk in the store where the post office is. So he learnt all about it when them fellers was a-coming and why. I'm telling you the truth. I ain't a bad feller, honest. I want to go straight. But I been scairt of Hamel. You won't let 'em hang me, will you, boys? Oh, and another thing. Hamel's been laughing all afternoon about the joke he played on Monroe near twenty years ago about that gambler, Diamond Jack O'Brien. It come up on account of you and your red hair. Hamel's been bragging how foxy he was to get Monroe to kill Diamond Jack and—"

Red interrupted emphatically. "No, you ain't a-going to be hung, Shorty. No, sir. You're going to be dragged by the heels right up to Mr. Monroe and made to tell him all you know, and if you don't persuade him it's gospel truth, you won't live long enough to get hung. He'll kill you sure! So you'd better be convincing. I'm going right up now and have a little talk with him first, then I'm coming down after you. And you, Mr. Waxman—there's a bunk in here. You'd better lay down."

"I'd like a drink, son."

"Whisky?"

"Water."

Red took a quart dipper from the water bucket and held it half filled to old Bill's mouth. He drank slowly.

"Son," he said slowly, "I won't hold a grudge agin anybody or feel bad if this all leads to Hamel getting his deserts. Hide'll grow back on my feet

Schmaling Mem. Pub. Library
501 Tenth Avenue
Fulton, IL 61252

and fingers. If Hamel and them Cross Bar fellers are run out of the country, Tajola'll be a pretty good cow country."

"Hamel may not know it," said Red, "but he's all the same as dead. Here—" Red backed up to old Bill—"hook yourself around my neck and let me get hold of your legs. You can lay in the bunk and listen to the music. There's going to be some along about sunup."

He carried old Bill pick-a-back into the room and gently let him slide down onto the bunk. Old Bill hung his feet over the end of it and held his hands elbow high in the air. That position seemed to ease the pain a little. Not a word of complaint passed his lips.

"One of the old-time breed, you are," said Red.

CHAPTER 17.

A Couple of Redheads

Just as he was leaving the kitchen, Red grabbed a cold boiled potato, hastily sprinkled it with salt, stuffed it into his mouth, and went out chewing. He was still hungry.

"After all them potatoes and steaks I've had, Mrs. Wyman ain't going to have much left over for hash. Most folks don't like hash, so I'm doing them a favor. Now, I wonder—will Monroe have some guns handy? Most likely not—not with his hip bones busted. Anyway, he's no danged outlaw to be scared by every footstep he hears. Besides, he can't hear mine. Ow, gosh!"

Red stopped, leaned against the wall in the dark, and rubbed at the sole of one foot and then the other. His socks had worn through. Bits of sand burrs had broken off and, as such things do, pricked at times with a needle-like sting. There was no way of getting them out.

He went on gingerly. In the hallway he stopped, listening, forgetful of stickers, holding both guns by the handles, ready to whip them out. He had heard footsteps, soft ones, stealthy, then low whispers.

"Now I wonder," he mused, "if they've got a notion they know where to find me? What else are they doing, nosing around here at 3 A.M.? I'll sure do my best to correct any such notions. Anyhow, this time of night all honest folks— 'cept me—ought to be in bed."

Red squatted low, waiting in the hallway below the stairs. He could not see anything and could hear nothing but the faint tiptoe step of stealthy men and the slight squeak of boards, with now and then a vague whisper. Red held his breath, not moving. Then he saw the dim outline of dark shapes, very hazily. Two men. They seemed to be coming into the hallway where he waited but paused at the foot of the stairs, then began to ascend. The stair steps creaked more than the floor. They swore under their breath. Red waited, patiently. He thought, "I bet a penny they're after me. I wonder what they think they'd do with me? Might be like the time I roped a bear. I learned a lot. Learned to leave my rope off bears. I burned my hands. The saddle turned and I got throwed off. The horse ran away and I climbed a tree. Fellers," he said in his own thoughts, turning his face upward in the darkness, "it's sure bad business to go looking for what you don't want to find."

Red did not move all the time they were on the stairs but peered overhead into the darkness, seeing nothing. Then he sniffed, a little puzzled, wrinkling his nose. In the still, hot air he had caught the tingling of a barbershop odor, bay rum.

There had been bay rum on those men. Who used bay rum? Punchers sometimes, when they came to town with three months' wages, went in, and had the barber put on all the fixings. But gamblers smelled of bay rum, always.

Red gasped noiselessly. "Those two gamblers? Then they're not looking for me. They're after Monroe. They've come like Shorty Crawley said to kill him and make folks think old Bill done it. If all Shorty says pans out truthful, I'm going to take it on myself to see he don't get hung."

Red knew that he would have to wait until the gamblers got off the stairs, even got into

Monroe's room, before he dared to start up—the squeaking under his feet would attract their attention—because he wanted Monroe to know that Hamel had sent them to kill him.

"That Hamel sure knows how to get other fellers to do his dirty work, now don't he? And think of hiring a post-office clerk to give you a feller's mail, then you steam it open, read it, seal it up, and give it back to the clerk. I wonder why it is skunks and such fellers seem so much smarter than other folks? Now, I'd never have thought of a thing like that."

As Red was waiting he heard the clatter of a horse's hoofs. It was not loud; it seemed far off. He cocked his ear alertly, but at that moment he vaguely heard Monroe's angry voice, then the jar of a closed door, and what Monroe said was cut off. The gamblers had quickly entered his room and shut the door.

Red jumped at the stairs. He was now afraid that he had done wrong to wait, afraid that the gamblers might kill Monroe quickly. He ran up the stairs on tiptoes, turned into the hall, and slowed down, moving cautiously. There were voices in Monroe's room, but they did not sound particularly angry. He slipped up, nearer and nearer, listening.

He could not hear very clearly but well enough to know that the gamblers were telling Monroe things. They had caught him crippled in bed, unarmed; and one of them in a thin mean voice was saying:

"You may have other fellows scared of you, but me and Perley, here, ain't. Tell Hamel to bring you our ears, will you! Why, Hamel brought us down here to Tajola to clean out punchers, his Cross Bar punchers 'specially, so he'd get back the wages he pays 'em and the cuts he gives 'em for stealing your cows. Your time's come, Monroe, and it might interest you to know—"

Red kicked open the door and stood there with both guns hip low and muzzles up. His eyes were blazing, but his mouth was twisted into a joyful grin. His hair was all tousled and poking out every which way; his face was bruised and blackened. At first glance, the gamblers seemed to think he was a devil and not a man. It took two winks for them to recognize him as the lanky puncher who had cut in on their game that night in the Cross Bar.

The younger gambler, the wolf-faced Timkins, who was doing the talking, held two guns in his delicate skinny hands. They were man-sized .45s with eight-inch barrels and the sights filed off; and Timkins wasn't used to a cowman's guns. They were old Bill's. Timkins had brought them, knowing that Monroe would have to be killed with a .45 if people were to think old Bill had done it. The gamblers had planned to shoot, jump down the dark stairs, out of the open front door, and away into the night before sleepy people would catch sight of them. Then the story would be told that old Bill and some friend who had helped him get out of the calaboose had come up and killed Monroe.

Perley Price, the fatter of the gamblers, held his gambler's gun, a short nickel-plated affair, good for killing men no farther off than across a card table.

Monroe, with all the bedclothes thrown off so there would not be the slightest weight on his broken hip, had raised himself up on an elbow, forgetful of his pain, and with grim, set face glared at Timkins. Monroe could look straight into any man's guns without batting an eye.

As Timkins said, "Your time's come . . ." Red had lifted up his foot and sent it against the weak latch of the door. The gamblers, with flinching, startled jerks, wheeled and stepped back, staring in amazement.

"Don't let me interrupt," said Red. "I'm curious, too—a heap."

They were armed, guns were in their hands, and he stood right before their eyes, filling the doorway; but they were afraid of him. They knew he was a killer, that he meant to kill them. They were gamblers and had cold nerve of a sort, but it wasn't the sort that jumped into a fight at point-blank range, not with a man who grinned as he waited for their first flicker of menace.

Red did not move—anything but his lips; and he said tauntingly, "Why don't you tell him Hamel put you up to killing him, then meant to make folks think old Bill broke jail and did it?"

They simply stared like frozen men. They wanted some flicker of advantage. They wouldn't, they simply couldn't, shoot it out gun to gun ith a man like Red. They knew he would kill them quicker than they could wink, and that he would shoot at the first twitch of movement. The muzzles of the heavy guns, to which Timkins was unaccustomed, sagged lower and lower. Fattish Perley Price, back of the skinny Timkins and almost behind him, licked his dry mouth as if about to speak but didn't.

"Why don't you tell him," Red added, "how you burned old Bill's feet and fingers, trying to make him tell where Mr. Monroe had his money hid—and old Bill wouldn't, even though Monroe, here, had turned against him?"

"Hamel put us up to it and was there," said the skinny Timkins. "And I ain't going to get killed for Hamel's doings."

With that he opened his hands, and let the guns fall. Knowing the range, he knew he was safe before Red if he dropped his guns.

"How about you, Fatty?" Red inquired.

Perley Price dropped his guns, too.

"I'm awful sorry it's against the law to shoot unarmed men," said Red. He added cheerfully,

"Still, it's all right to hang 'em, so you card stealers won't feel plumb neglected. You must still be wearing your holdout, Fatty, 'cause you ain't lifting your hands much now, neither."

Perley Price put up his hands shoulder high.

"Hand me up one of them guns," said Monroe. "I've got no feelings against shooting 'em, unarmed or loaded down with cannons."

"Nope," said Red. "You see, Mr. Monroe—" He turned his head for a quick glance at Monroe, and as if that one look aside were a signal, Timkins, with flip of hand, jerked at his own nickel-plated affair that he wore in a spring holster under his coat; and at the same instant, Perley Price, with down-drop and scrambling back movement of body, so as to get into the shelter of the bed, grabbed at his gun.

Timkins, by long practice of nervous card-trained fingers, was quick as a flash. As he drew, he jumped sideways, and though his gun went off, the noise of it was not heard, for the roar of Red's .45 seemed to gobble up the very sound of the smaller gun which pitched its bullet at the ceiling. But Timkins went down with lead in his heart and his evil face set in a noiseless gasp.

With flick of thumb Red also shot almost simultaneously with his second gun. Natural gifts and long training made him use his guns almost as effortlessly, as instinctively, as he used his fingers; but as the hammer was falling he was

189

stabbed with fear and jerked his hand, sending the shot wild.

The crippled Monroe, with a heave of his body and a kick of his uninjured leg, had thrown himself out of the bed on top of the gambler who, crouching knees down, had scrambled into shelter, meaning to shoot Red from behind cover.

Red, by an almost clairvoyant sense, such as gunmen seem to have, had shot at where he *knew* the gambler's head was. Probably too quick for thought he had seen from the corner of his eyes that the gambler's head was there; and he had shot even as he looked more directly—and as he looked the hammer was falling. But it was no longer the gambler's head, but Monroe's back, that he saw.

With no more than the hundredth part of a second to spare, Red acted. The bullet struck the floor. Red jumped forward with gun held to strike the gambler's head, but there was nothing to be seen of it.

Monroe was on him. Tugging and jerking, their bodies swayed. There was the snarl of quick, hot breathing, broken curses from the gambler. A kind of thin smoke rose from the dusty floor. Monroe was practically helpless from the hips down. The gambler bucked and writhed. Their struggling moved the bed. Red hopped about, unable to do anything and swearing vaguely.

Then there was a muffled report. And another.

The bodies sank, Monroe still on top of the gambler, as if both were dead.

Red pulled at Monroe's shoulder, speaking to him anxiously. "Mr. Monroe?"

Monroe, breathing hoarsely, lifted his head. His tone was quiet, but the sentence was broken with gasps. "I'm all right—when I get my breath. The doctor said—said I might never ride again—if I didn't keep quiet but—but I had to kill him—with his own gun."

Monroe had got his fingers on the gun and, pressing it against Perley Price's body, had shot, twice.

"Gee gosh!" said Red. "I thought you'd been shot, too."

Monroe raised his head higher, pushed, trying to rise, and with a hand out-groping, felt for the bed. "You would have cared?" he asked calmly. "You know, don't you, I offered a reward for your head?"

"Hell, I don't care how many rewards are offered for my head—long as nobody collects. The fact is, this is an awful mix-up, Mr. Monroe, but I ain't done nothing much wrong. Just let me help you get into bed and I'll—"

Red, hearing steps, wheeled with gun set. A tall angular form filled the doorway. The man there, showing no interest at all in Red's gun, said in slow, solemn voice, "It appears like always I manage to come too slow for the show."

"For the love of Pete's grandmother, Buck! Where'd you come from?"

Old Buck Waxman straightened up a little and stepped in, looking down at Monroe.

"Mrs. Morgan," said Buck, "sent word out to me that hell sure had busted loose here in town, so I come to help this fool kid, here, face the music."

Monroe, in great pain, angered, mystified, and still struggling to rise on his one good leg, demanded savagely, "What the hell have you been up to? Damned dirty work, it looks like, and crooked, too. I want to know!"

Red put away his guns and helped Monroe, saying, "It may not be all right, what me and Buck have got into, but there's no dirty work about it. You just set down there and listen."

But before Buck could start talking, the hotel's four or five lodgers, together with Mrs. Wyman, having been aroused by the shots, came crowding into the hall. Their eyes were popping; their tongues buzzed with questions. Mrs. Wyman caught sight of Buck Waxman and squawked, "Whatever's happened, it's all right. Buck's here."

Buck sidled off awkwardly, mumbling, "It was all right before I got here, Mrs. Wyman. Red and Monroe have sent them gamblers to the happy hunting ground."

"Happy hunting, hell!" said Red. "They're a foot deep under grease in the devil's skillet. Listen. All you folks crowd in here and listen to what me and Buck's got to say to Mr. Monroe."

"Can't you tell it private?" said Monroe.

"Nosir. You went and made it gosh-darn public that me and Buck had rigged a flim-flam game on you, so folks have got a right to know. I ain't much good as a liar. I ain't been much of one, either. I came to town looking for work. I ate supper and walked down to the Cross Bar Saloon, where I met Buck coming out. We stood and talked about nothing in particular, then I went in. Them gamblers—these gamblers—" Red swept a hand at the bodies—"were trimming a red-headed boy of about my own size and age. From certain symptoms, I suspected they were using a holdout. So I cut in and said, 'Hands up!' The gamblers gave the kid back his money. Then me and Buck came up here to the hotel and talked some more, then Buck went to bed in the next room. Then that red-headed kid followed me up to my room and says he's a heap grateful and for me to look out because the gamblers and Hamel are laying to plug me. I ask the kid his name and he says to call 'im Smith. I spot that as a hair brand of a name and said so. Then he ups and says he'll tell me something. He says his name is Jerome Douglas, but—"

"What's that?" Monroe shouted.

"You lay still and listen. You're going to hear it all, Mr. Monroe. He says his mother's dead and the cow outfit where he's been raised, up in Colorado, has been sold. He says some time ago he got a letter, and it sure is a curious one. It says, 'You don't know nothing about who you are or your dad, but I know all about you. And I think maybe I can do something nice for the family. You come down here to Tajola, give out that your name is Frank Peters, loaf around a day or two, and I'll look you up.'

"Well, the kid came but he got cold feet about giving out that his name was Peters. He wants to look around some first, so he says his name is Smith.

"While I'm setting there, reading the letter, Shorty Crawley comes knocking at my door and tells me Buck, here, has been hurt down at the Stage barn and wants to see me. Buck is snoring in the next room, so I know why they want to see me down to the barn. I leave the kid to ride herd on Crawley and I go. I go the back way and sneak in, set and listen. Then a feller comes running down to the barn to say they've shot *me* with a rifle through the window of my room. I know right off it's the kid they've shot, and that makes me hot under the collar, so I wade in and talk to 'em. Well, sir, when the smoke's clearing away, there's Mr. Monroe riding in slow an' calm.

"He talks some and asks me my name. All of a sudden I get the fool notion that the kid being dead, maybe I ought to take the name of Frank Peters just to see what was going to happen to him. So I did.

194

"When I get back up here to the hotel and tell Buck what all has happened, he wiggles uncomfortable-like, tells me that there boy is Mr. Monroe's son, and that he, Buck, had meant to get the kid down here, put him to work on the Zee Zee, let Mr. Monroe get to like him, and maybe take a fancy to him. Buck says Mr. Monroe's awful touchy about folks meddling with his personal affairs. Besides he wants the kid taken care of right, so he lights out and tells Mrs. Morgan to come in here and get the boy.

"Well, sir, she is driven in by a feller named Harry Stow, who's known me since I was wearing diapers. All unintentional, he tells folks my name is Red Clark. Mr. Monroe somehow must have got hold of that letter Buck had written the kid telling him to come down here as Frank Peters, so he up and suspicioned me as an imposticator and wanted my hide to nail on his barn door. That's the truth, every word of it—excepting that I've left out a lot. But Hamel is an ornery skunk of a man who's been lying to you, Mr. Monroe, and stealing from you, and pulling the wool over your eyes for twenty years.

"What's more, when he learned about me not being who you thought I was, it gave him the bright idea of having you killed so he could run in somebody as your son and get the Zee Zee. And them gamblers came up here to do it.

"Buck's brother, old Bill—Mr. Monroe, he

didn't know a thing on earth about what me and Buck here had done. You judged him clear wrong. Down there in the calaboose, Hamel and these here gamblers burned his fingers and feet to make him tell where you kept your money. And he wouldn't. I got him out. He's downstairs now in the kitchen. Shorty Crawley is there, too, all tied up in a knot and just busting to tell the truth. Some of you folks go down and drag him up here so Mr. Monroe can listen."

Mrs. Wyman said, "For land sakes!" Men made explosive comments in amazement. They stared at Red, they stared at Buck, but looked longest and steadiest at Mr. Monroe. He was a stubborn man, with a sort of iron mask of a face. Pain gnawed at his broken hip. He was angered and yet in some ways he was not angry. He peered at Red from under drawn eyebrows. He did not doubt Red's story.

Monroe asked slowly, "That was my boy that was bad hurt?"

"Yessir, I reckon so."

"Then you tell the doctor to get out to Morgan's ranch and stay there till my boy is cured!" said Monroe, letting go of his emotions and speaking as he felt.

"But you need the doctor yourself," Mrs. Wyman protested.

"Damn myself! I want that boy taken care of!"

CHAPTER 18.

At Sunup

Some of the men partly carried and partly dragged Shorty Crawley up the stairs into Monroe's room where, with a good deal of shivering as if half frozen, he sat bound in a chair and talked.

Buck had stayed down in the kitchen to talk with his brother, and there Red found him.

"Listen, Buck. It's almost sunup. You and me have some work to do. When Crawley gets through talking, word of what he's told'll be all over town. Hamel'll light out. I'm going after his scalp."

"He sleeps over to the Cross Bar, upstairs," said Buck, rising from the edge of the bunk where his brother lay.

"He ain't asleep now. Hell! He's waiting for those gamblers to come back. That's why we've got to get a wiggle on."

Old Bill spoke up from the bunk. "You two want to go slow and be careful. A lot of his Cross Bar rustlers are there. He sent for 'em just in case there was to be some trouble here in town."

"We'll be careful not to waste no bullets, won't we, Buck?"

"Unh," said Buck. Just an uninterested grunt. A pause. Then, "Morgan and his riders are coming into town. I lit out ahead. He says Monroe or no Monroe, he's going to clean that Cross Bar outfit off the range."

"Well, let's be going," Red urged. "We don't want to wait for help."

Buck grunted again, then paused before he spoke. "When you've lived to be as old as me, kid, you'll have learned to slow down in your anxiety to get into trouble. Go slow and shoot first. That's my motto. Also, have a horse handy in case you need him. You may need him to chase the other fellow with. My horse is wore out. We'll go down to the barn and get a couple."

"We don't need no horses."

"Hamel's foxy. Supposing he gets a-horseback and goes off, leaving us to walk."

"All right. Have it your way. But come on."

"It's a miracle to me," said Buck sadly, speaking partly to his brother, partly to Red, "how kids ever live long enough to get themselves some sense. They're always so hasty to get into trouble. We've got plenty of time."

"We ain't. Hamel's waiting for them gamblers. If they don't show up, he's going to get nervous. She's almost daylight."

"'Tain't," said Buck. "But all right, then. Let's make a start. S'long, Bill."

"S'long, Buck. S'long, son," said Bill. "Have a good time."

"Well, one thing's dead certain," said Red, sticking up a foot. "I ain't going to die with my boots on." He rubbed at the sole of the foot, adding, "I darned near died already a couple of times from having 'em off. But shucks, I got no right to whine over stepping in cactus when I'm talking to a man who let 'em burn the hide right off his feet rather than tell. Me, if I'd had a million dollars hid somewhere, I'd tell 'em to let my toes alone and go get it."

"Yes," said old Bill slowly. "I've seen how easy you give up—me and Hellbender, we both saw."

Buck spoke up sarcastically. "I thought you was in a hurry to get some place."

As they stepped out of the kitchen Red said, "You got on boots. I'm going to ride down to the barn."

"All right, you ride along. Saddle a couple of good horses. I'll be along by the time you're ready."

Old Buck was as casual about it, and sounded just about as indifferent, as if they were to saddle a couple of horses to ride out and look for strays. Red climbed into the saddle of the weary horse which had carried Buck and rode off. Over his shoulder in the hazy starlight he saw the old man coming along at a slow, half-sidling gait, not hurrying in the least.

"If I didn't know that old gazebo," said Red to himself, "I'd think he wasn't anxious to entertain himself by blowing smoke in folks's faces."

Red rode into the barn with the bridle reins in his teeth and a gun in each hand. He didn't know what he was likely to meet. It was dark, totally dark, inside the barn's wide doorway. He jerked back his head, pulling on the reins, and the horse stopped. Red waited, expecting a hail from the man on duty. There was not a sound but the faint rattle of a halter rope and the idle stomp of a horse or two.

"Well," mused Red, just the least little bit ashamed, as he poked his guns away, "looks like for once I was acting scared all for no good reason. But it's mighty helpful at times to be a little scared—though you do feel like a fool when 'tain't necessary."

He sang out with a loud, "Hey-oh, there! Fetch me a light."

The echo of his voice rang through the barn, but there was no answer.

"Ain't nobody to home, I reckon," he said, and tossed the reins to the ground as he swung off.

He knew just about where to find a lantern and looked up as he scratched a match. The lantern was just above his hand when a voice from the darkness across the passageway called sharply, "Hands up!"

All in an instant Red flung the match one way

200

and jumped the other, falling to knees and elbows but facing about with a gun out. No shot was fired. Red, unconsciously and by good luck, had jumped behind the horse; and the lighted match he had thrown had fallen in the dusty passage- way that was littered with straw. The tiny flame nibbled at the loose hay, casting a flickering light, and the fire began to spread with a quick nibble at the dried grass about it.

Red had scarcely hit the ground before he was up. With quick snatch of left hand he checked the horse, pulling its head around, and with the other he leveled his gun across the saddle at a dim figure barely seen by the flickering light.

"Drop your guns and get to fighting fire, or I'll roast you alive, feller," said Red. "You dang well know you can't hit me," he added, half jeering, half in earnest. "And you know dang well I can hit you. I'm near the door, so I won't burn to death, but you—come on! Shoot or fight fire."

A moment's hesitation, a sullen oath, then the soft thud of something falling, and the figure that had become slightly more distinct with the fire's widening circle stepped out with hands up.

The man wore only one holster.

"All right, get busy stomping and kicking dirt on the fire. Use your hat. Act like you were an Injun doing a war dance. Hustle! Jump up and down. Use your hat, I told you!"

Red stepped out and also scraped dust at the

widening circle of tiny flames, but he was barefooted—or the same as barefooted, for his socks were worn through—and the ash was hot. He jumped back, wiping his foot in the cool dust.

"Use your *hat,* feller, *and don't burn those boots!* They look like they might fit me."

Buck Waxman cautiously poked his head around the barn doorway, took a careful look, and stepped inside. He asked with melancholy petulance, "Now what you up to? Gosh blame, but I can't leave you out of my sight a minute but what you start a ruckus."

"We got company, Buck. He's doing an Injun fire dance for me. Use your hat, I told you. Light a lantern, will you, Buck? Then you might help him put out this here little fire."

Buck saw that the broken circle of tiny flame could easily become serious. He quickly lit a lantern and, snatching a blanket from one of the many saddles, began to beat the ground.

Red looked on critically and talked.

"You can be really spry for a feller that'd have gray in his beard—if he had a beard. Buck, I rode in here all loaded for bear with both guns out and the reins in my teeth, like a picture-book hero. Nary a sound. I set and listened. All was quiet. I sung out. Nobody spoke. Then I crawled off and reached for a lantern, and this hombre opened his mouth and scared the pee-wadding out of me. Say, you, why didn't you shoot when I jumped?"

The fire was out. The man stood dusty, sweating, and sullen, eyeing Red from under downcast lids.

"I asked you a question," Red insisted. "Why didn't you shoot?"

"Aw, go to hell," said the man sourly.

"I'm curious, that's all."

"You jumped too quick. That's all. I wasn't expecting it. I thought you'd turn around—"

"And stand still?" Red interrupted. "You haven't been out West long, you haven't. When you didn't shoot, I knew I had you licked. What you doing down here, anyhow?"

"I wanted that thousand dollars Monroe offered. That's all. I figured that you was hiding here in town, and that before morning you'd slip down here after a horse. All the horses was brought down here a little after twelve tonight. I just thought I'd outguess the other fellers that's up to the Cross Bar drinking. When you come in on horseback I couldn't figure it was you. But when you lit that match I just—Well, I never thought any man could jump that fast." A pause, then grudgingly, " 'Tain't human."

Red grinned. "Feller, I got training as a kid jumping bushes where I thought a locust was a rattler. You by happenchance working for Hamel?"

"No. I just rode in yesterday looking for work. I seen you ride this morning, and I heard the talk. I need money bad, and I figured you'd sure come down after a horse before morning. That's all."

"How long you been out West here?"

" 'Bout three year."

"That's two more'n I'd have guessed. My gosh, feller, I come awful near to plugging you. Listen, after this when you pull a gun, use it if the other feller so much as wrinkles his nose. I'm talking for your own good. Now, where's the barn boss?"

"There ain't been anyone down here. I been here all alone since about midnight."

"Buck, this here gentleman needs some money bad. I ain't got none. But see if you can't persuade him for to loan me his boots. I'm going to saddle up."

Red took another lantern. He looked observantly at the saddles and counted them. From them he judged that there were about six or seven of Hamel's Cross Bar riders in town.

The horse in the nearest stall was the one that had been kept up to bring in the others from the pasture. The next was Hellbender, standing just where Red had tied him along about noon the day before.

"Hello, you old devil," said Red from the next stall, holding the lantern up, peering at the vicious horse. "I reckon nobody was kind-hearted enough to get themselves kicked to death by trying to turn you out to pasture. Do you remember me?"

Red slowly put out his hand. Hellbender jerked back. Red leaned over, reaching. He touched the horse's cheek, stroking it, talking.

"We're friends, you know. Leastwise I want to be friends, always, with anybody that can lick me."

Hellbender with sullen uneasiness let himself be patted. At least, he did not snap.

"Sure you remember me. I'm that little red-headed boy that was lucky enough to land in the saddle every time you sent him kiting. I made dints in my saddle seat where I lit."

When Red led out Hellbender, Buck was standing there with a pair of boots in his hands and the other man, in his stocking feet, leaned against a post, looking sour.

"Kid, you ain't going to ride that horse tonight," Buck said earnestly.

"I am if he'll let me. He's got sense, this horse. He says to me, just now, he says, 'Red, you're a nice boy, and I know there ain't no use trying to throw any man that has got ears like yours. You just spread 'em like they was wings and flap right back into the saddle.' Yessir, that's what he said. Didn't you, Heller?"

As Red talked he was busily saddling; and Hellbender took it, quite as if he had expressed just the sentiments that Red claimed.

While Buck was pulling off his saddle and putting it on the other horse, Red tried on the boots and stamped his feet down into them.

"My feet slosh about like they was a couple of lone oysters in two soup bowls. But they'll have to do, I reckon, spurs an' all. Did you pay the feller, Buck?"

Buck grunted.

"Hell, you've got to pay him. I don't want him to think I'm a thief. Besides, if I was going to steal boots, I'd get myself a better fit than these."

Red crossed over to where the man's gun had fallen. He picked it up, wiped off the dust, looked at it curiously. It was a gun that broke. Red broke it, dumping the shells into his hands. He eyed them, poking with his forefinger.

"Baby bullets," he said, and flung them into the dust. "Feller, a word of parting. Here's your gun. I'm being friendly. If you want to live long enough to have some grandchildren 'round your knee, get out of this country. I'm not being funny or insulting. I'm telling you. You were hatched back East, and it ain't in your blood. Me and Buck would maybe look as silly in your home town as you do in ours. But any man that's as slow to shoot as you, and carries a .38 in a .45 country—he's just naturally begging to get bunged up."

With that Red broke off, leading Hellbender out of the barn. Being proud of having delivered his little lecture, he swung into the saddle sort of forgetfully, and Hellbender went into the air. Red, not giving an exhibition now, promptly grabbed the horn, jerked up the horse's head, and said things. But after a stiff-legged caper or two, Hellbender seemed to remember that this man was his master and stood still.

Old Buck rode up close and drawled, sadly and sarcastically, "You trying to pull that horn out by the roots or something, like it was a sore tooth?"

"Say, you listen. If you want to know how nice it is to have a saddle horn to hold to, we'll swap horses right here and now. I rode this here horse once today, free and clean and I ain't been so dang sore since my dad paddled me for saying I hadn't been into the sugar bowl when it was sticking all 'round my mouth. What we going to do now? Ride right into the Cross Bar and make some noise?"

"No, we ain't. I'm going in the front way and you go 'round back and—"

"You guessed wrong. I'm going in the front way, and *you* can go around back and set on your tail till the doings is done."

"Now, kid, this is my show. I got a little piece I want to speak to them Cross Bar fellers, so you—"

"I'll march right in with you and listen."

"And let Hamel and them bolt out the back way?"

"Men you shoot at first don't bolt much of any way—'cept head first to hell."

"All right," said Buck, "we'll toss a coin."

"It'll be your coin. I'm too near broke to run the risk of droppin' my four bits in the road."

Buck fumbled in his pocket, pitched a coin lightly, caught it, and asked, "What you take?"

"I always take heads."

Buck leaned forward, peering in the starlight at his palm. "Tails win," he said calmly, putting the coin back into his pocket.

"I smell me a shenanigan, you old shitepoke, you!" Red then hastily plucked a coin from his pocket, put it into his palm, and bent forward, peering. "You couldn't see whether it was head or tails. You just took a quick peek and flim-flammed me."

"You going to welsh?"

"Was it tails—honest?"

"I think so," said Buck calmly. "Like you said, in the dark I couldn't see very clear, but I didn't see no head so I judged it must be tails."

"All right, then, I'll go the back way if you promise to wait till I get up close enough to hear your little speech."

"Now listen. You get off and leave your horse down the alley a couple hundred feet, then you stay there near the back way. Some of them fellers may break through. If they do, they'll make a bee line to the corral for horses. We'll just hop in the saddle and catch 'em. She's going to start to get light in about twenty minutes or less. Now go slow and limber. I'm to make my speech first."

CHAPTER 19.

The Fight at the Cross Bar

In the Cross Bar Saloon a half dozen men who were tired, a little drunk, and irritable, hung about the bar, fiddle-faddled with cards, or half dozed. They had been under a strain, waiting up all night, expecting something to happen. Hamel had told them big medicine was being made. He had said Monroe was bad hurt, might not live, and if he died—why, then, a lot of things would happen. They understood clearly enough what he meant, for they weren't honest cowmen. Hamel wouldn't have honest men working for him. The men who did work for him made so much money that he wasn't satisfied to get it back over his bar and through faro. He had brought in a couple of card sharks. These were hard men, mostly on the dodge, and any one of them would have been hanged if the other cowmen of Tajola had known their tricks.

Now they loafed about wearily. Some tried to talk with Slim the barkeep and pump him a bit for he was close to Hamel. But Slim was tired, too, close-mouthed and irritable. They had all talked out every subject they had to talk about.

"Where the hell is Hamel?" said Tom Jugg, a

squat fellow with a knife gash on the side of his face. "I bet he's gone up and gone to sleep."

"He hauled us a-hopping into town with word that something was goin' to happen, and it ain't," said Larry Flint, disgusted. "I'd like to have laid my eyes on that there Red feller."

"Them that has is mostly sleeping peaceful," said Slim, spreading out an old newspaper on the bar and leaning forward.

"Where is Hamel? Upstairs?" Jugg repeated.

"Oh, him and Shane's holding a powwow," said Henry Cary. Shane was the Cross Bar foreman.

At that moment Blinky Thomas came hurrying in with jangle of spurs.

"Where's Hamel?" he called. "Where's Hamel?"

"What's bit you?" asked Jugg.

"Where's Hamel, Slim? Where is he?" Blinky's voice was high-pitched.

Slim leaned on the newspaper and eyed Blinky. "What's your rush?"

"He sent me down to the calaboose to see about Bill Waxman—and he's gone. Him and Crawley, too. Gone."

Men stirred at that, shifting about alertly, looked questioningly at Slim.

"He's upstairs with Shane. You'd better go up and tell him," said Slim.

Blinky, important at carrying news, trotted through the saloon and up the back stairs. The jangle and clank of spurs and boots were heard, and Shane opened the door before Blinky reached it.

Shane was thin, muscular, dark, tricky, but no coward. He and Hamel were not exactly drunk, but pretty well loaded from drinking as they joyfully planned how to take full advantage of their good luck.

"What's your rush?" Shane asked as Blinky stopped before him.

"Waxman's gone! And Crawley, too!"

"Gone!" said Shane.

"Gone!" Hamel echoed, coming forward with head out-thrust as if by sticking his ears forward he could hear the quicker.

"Gone," said Blinky.

Shane and Hamel stared, each at the other. Hamel pulled at his fat jaw nervously. Shane's fingers twitched at the handle of a gun, then with sudden thought he looked at his watch.

"Good God!" he exclaimed. "It's morning!" He turned toward the window. The first gray misty light of the coming dawn vaguely brightened the earth. "We been setting here drinking an' forgetting—"

Hamel swore, deep-throated, furious. "Them gamblers, put it over on us! They killed Monroe, they made off with old Bill. And Crawley throwed in with 'em! They've lit out for the ranch to get that money Monroe's got hid! We been jigger-rooed!"

"Shh!" said Shane, pushing Blinky aside, and stepping into the hall. "Don't I hear—downstairs—Listen!"

Old Buck Waxman, just as calmly as if he were coming in to have a couple of drinks, had stepped through the wide-open doors of the Cross Bar. The first flush of morning was lightly touching the eastern sandhills. The cool freshness of dawn was in the air. Lamps were still burning in the saloon.

Old Buck with slope-shouldered, sidling gait came in and twiddled the ends of his drooping mustache with thumb and forefinger of his left hand as he glanced about. Then his hand fell and he stood still and eyed the men one after another with a half-mournful gaze.

They had stiffened alertly, sidling this way and that, letting their hands fall. They knew Buck was bad medicine, but their eyes shifted uneasily past him toward the vague darkness beyond the doorway. They could not believe that he had walked in on them alone.

"Howdy," said Buck.

A voice or two answered with inarticulate grunts.

Slim, with a very idle sort of movement had reached for the long stick and was quietly lifting it toward the ceiling, ready to tap a signal overhead.

"If I was you, Slim, I'd set that pole back down,"

said Buck in a low drawl, with no excitement, not even much earnestness in his tone. The tip of his thumbs hung at the edge of his belt. Other men thumbed their belts, and some, palms turned backwards and arms low, waited.

"When I get ready!" said Slim.

"Well, you are ready, right now, ain't you?" Buck asked it with a sort of pleading mildness, but there was no more than the corner of his eye on Slim. In fact, his eyes looked rather blank as if he were not looking at anybody in particular, which meant that he was watching every man there.

Slim put down the pole.

"I been moseyin' 'round on the range some the last month or two," said Buck, as if speaking to himself, "and I find that quite a considerable number of cows has been trailed over the back country 'cross Lost Canyon and—"

"Say, what the hell are you getting at?" Jugg shouted.

"Me? Oh, I just thought maybe you boys would be interrested to know that the Mexican buyer of them cows held out two dollars a head on you and gave it to Hamel sort of secret-like as his rake-off."

"Why, damn his lousy soul," said Larry Flint. "I suspicioned Hamel—"

"Steady there, steady," said Slim. "Don't you see he's up to tricks?"

213

"All the tricks I'm up to," said Buck slowly, "is to make Monroe know what Hamel's doing and has been doing all these years. You boys can back him up if you want. I had a talk with the Mexican buyer some days back, and he told me things. But his evidence ain't no good, seeing as how for one thing he is a Mexican, and for another he is dead. Most of what I want in this world is for Monroe to know that Hamel is a dirty, lying, sneaking rustler and an all-'round thief. I didn't come here alone to make my little speech. This dump is surrounded, plentiful. So you boys can take your choice. Stick up for Hamel and maybe—most likely—get bad hurt, or agree to tell Monroe the truth, then so-journ for a spell in the penitentiary."

Having said his little piece, Buck waited as mildly blissful and contented as a man with four aces watching other folks fingering their chips to raise the pot. He had them more than halfway bluffed. With anxious eyes peering through the dim doorway they seemed to see shadow shapes, with drawn guns, waiting for a signal. They just couldn't believe that he had walked in on them alone—one man facing six, with Slim making an evil seventh. The very audacity of Buck's coming carried conviction.

Some men glanced back to the rear of the saloon, half expecting to see Buck's friends there. Fingers twitched toward gun handles and fell away. Half furtive, questioning glances went from face to face, each man hopeful to see what the next felt like doing.

"We're covered, boys, and ain't got a chance," said a husky voice, and the man raised his hands.

"That's sensible," said Buck, just as calmly as the man with four aces might watch a fellow with two pairs throw away his hand. "Now who's next?"

Men hesitated nervously. Buck had got them in the chill gray dawn. The whisky, idly drunk through the long night, had lost its nip and soured in their stomachs. Earlier in the night their hands would have leaped gunward and contemptuous curses, would have crackled on their lips. But now Buck had caught them at low ebb. He had poisoned their fighting spirit by telling how Hamel had double-crossed them with his secret rake-off. Another man half lifted his hands, hesitating, not quite sure whether or not to put them up.

"By God," said Jugg, "I don't know about goin' to the pen—again."

At that moment there was the thump, thump, thump of quick boot heels on the stairs, the long-legged scrape of spurs. As he came from out the shadows of the saloon's rear, Shane shouted, "What the hell?"

Answering him, Slim yelled, "He's running a blazer!" at the same instant ducking low behind the bar. There with hasty reach he grabbed a rifle and jabbed it toward the knothole, carefully left for just such emergency. Shane unhesitatingly shot. Also the rifle boomed with belch of smoke. Men shouted vaguely, swearing as they went into action. And they learned why old Buck Waxman dared to run his blazer, almost lone-handed— quite lone-handed, in fact, for Red, in the misty darkness of the alley, had for a minute or two mistaken the restaurant next door for the back of the Cross Bar.

Waxman's hands flicked at his guns. They were out and going, hip low, as quickly as a snake strikes. His thumbs waggled at the hammers of his triggerless guns. A sort of pounding roar, with now and then the bigger boom of the .38-.40 that, almost blindly, was poked through the knothole, filled the barnlike saloon. Echoes rattled the very glasses on the shelf back of the bar. A dozen guns were blazing, and smoke, fog thick, spun about men who shot half blindly. Some man with upward sweep of gun barrel knocked out the nearest lamp, then splashed forward with long leap, face first, to the floor. Tom Jugg, with one arm broken, went belly down to peer beneath the smoke, and a bullet took him almost squarely through the tip-top crown of his hat. A bullet crashed through the pine boarding under the bar and the .38-.40 ceased firing while Sam, with a face full of splinters and a bullet near the top of his breast, coughed and writhed, clutching wildly at his neck. Wild shots smashed into the bottles and glass behind the bar, adding the clatter of falling glassware to the racket.

Men cursed wildly, some dying, some trying to run with lead in their bellies. Tables were thrown over in the panic, and there was the stumble and thump of men who dropped, badly hurt. Shane's voice rose loud in anger, bullets splattered about Buck like pebbles thrown by the handful.

There was a slackening of gunfire as this man and that went out of the fight, but a thickening of smoke.

Old Buck, hit through the shoulder, backed to the wall. Struck in the leg, he leaned more heavily on the boarding. Hit through the breast, he threw back his head, yet his wiry thumbs snapped at the hammers until they clicked, empty. Then face down, he fell and with scrambling, clawlike groping dragged himself to where Tom Jugg lay dead. With Jugg's gun, Buck went on shooting.

At the first burst of shooting Red had jumped for the back door of the Cross Bar, slammed it wide open and slid through. He paused, peering into the smoke haze blotted by the vague shapes of men up near the bar. The winking lash of gunfire popped like scattered firecrackers. In a half second's peering he made out old Buck by the flame of his guns. They were the only guns that were shooting toward the back of the saloon. Red cut loose, right and left, then a bullet that

217

seemed to come from the ceiling fairly singed his hair. He spun about with the quick scramble of a cat on a slate roof, and before his feet had paused in their motion he had shot once, then again, at a dim figure above him that leaned with leveled gun across the stair's railing. Blinky Thomas crumpled up and came bumping down the steep stairs, rolling over and over and over like a drunken man.

Red, peering overhead, thought he saw another shape but wasn't sure. He did not want to waste a bullet on the shadow. He waited watchfully a long second or two, then he heard Shane's angry shout, turned, running forward, shooting as he went. For a moment or two guns seemed going off in every direction. The second light had been shot out, and smoke filled the big, almost windowless saloon. Dawn had come, but the dimness of a dark twilight was upon them. The shooting slackened off. Nearly every man was dead or badly hit. Groans and curses mingled, and there was the scrape of spur and boot as some man who couldn't stand dragged himself aimlessly, not knowing which way to go but trying to escape. Then two guns went off almost simultaneously and nearly point-blank to each other.

A heavy thud followed. The shooting had stopped.

Red stood tense and peering. It seemed to him that he waited a long half hour, though he knew that it was probably a full minute at most.

He called, "Hi, Buck?" No answer. Only vague groans and mumblings and curses. The crippled man had stopped his crawling. He had come to a wall and lay there. Red shifted on tiptoes just in case some man with a gun was trying to place him by the sound of his voice, and called again, "Buck?"

No answer. Even the groaning men were losing their voices. Stillness, like a presence, seemed to be coming into the saloon. The smoke sifted about, and with wisplike wavering showed the clear light of morning through the wide-open front doorway.

"Buck! Buck, are you hurt?"

No answer. Red swore vaguely. What he meant was a kind of prayer. After the terrific reverberant roar of many guns the silence was oppressive. Red, who had camped alone for weeks, not missing companionship, now felt suddenly lonely. He stood in the midst of dead and dying men; and fear told him that Buck was among them.

"Buck! Damn it, Buck!"

No answer. The smoke swirled in a cloudy\ draft through the doorways, both of which were wide open. As it lifted from the floor, drifting up and out, Red stirred, bending to peer at this body and that, searching for what he hoped he would not find.

Near the bar he found Buck, face down, one arm

half out and gun still in his hand. Almost head to head with him lay Shane, the Cross Bar foreman. With his last shot each had killed the other.

Red dropped to his knees, tugging at Buck, pulling him over, hoping for life. There was none. He stared into the wrinkled, sad gray face and brokenly cursed the men who lay dead, all about. The lot of them were not worth Buck's little finger.

With a kind of sense of waking up, Red became aware that people were about the door, and there was a vague soft staccato drumming in his ears. He looked up, listening. Horses, coming on the run, coming fast, with clatter of hoofs.

Red turned, still on his knees and with drawn guns, faced the doorway where townspeople had begun to swarm as flies come to dead meat. He was angered to the point of downright madness, and words rippled over his lips with the sound of curses.

"Stand back out of here, you yellow dogs! If you'd had the grit of a sick pup you'd've cleaned Hamel and his gang out of here long ago. And you, you lousy sheriff, if you still want me, go up to Monroe and ask him. And you long-tailed judge, you, get to where I can't see you. It took a man to do the work you—the lot of you—ought to have done with a rope long ago. And they killed him!"

Red's voice rang with the truth of what he said,

and men flinched. Storekeepers turned their eyes in accusing stares at the bleary-eyed sheriff and muttered so the judge could overhear.

The pounding of horsemen who came at a furious gallop was in the street, before the saloon, and there stopped with abrupt stiff-legged skittering. Over the heads of the crowd in the doorway Red caught a blurred glimpse of men in saddles. He heard their sharp, quick questions. Then with heavy stride the horsemen pushed the crowd aside and pressed in behind a tall gray man who stopped short with a backward jerk of body as he saw that Red held, though he did not raise, a gun.

"Who the hell are you!" Red snapped.

"Morgan."

Red stood up, thrust the gun away, and pointed down. "You've been a long time getting here. There he is—he did it all himself."

Morgan came forward, looked down into old Buck's upturned face, pulled off his hat, then turned slowly, gazing at the dead men strewn about on the saloon floor. Morgan's men, with uncovered heads, stared about and muttered in astonishment.

"All of 'em—lone-handed?"

"There's one out back somewhere that I dropped. The rest are his. There's no other man alive that would have walked in on 'em like he did. He made me go the back way. Said they might bolt. Bolt, hell!"

"We rode to the Cross Bar Ranch," said Morgan, "and found out almost everybody was here in town. So we came, knowing something was up." He moved his hand, indicating the bodies, and asked, "Is Hamel one of 'em?"

"He'd better be or I'll chase him from here to China to choke him with lead."

Morgan's riders moved about, looking from one dead man to another. Two were still alive but unconscious.

"You," said Morgan, peering hard, "are the Clark boy?"

"Yes."

"I know about everything. Buck told me."

"Yes, we used the same blanket, me and him, lots of times. He was a man."

"Mr. Morgan," said a rangy, bow-legged, sun-blackened young fellow, speaking sort of reluctantly, "Hamel don't appear to be here, and that's a fact."

"Then find him!" said Morgan. "Scatter and find him."

"Holy gosh," said Red wearily, taking a deep sigh as he shifted his belt, settled the holsters, "now I got to stay in this damn country till that skunk's buried."

He began prodding out empty shells and reloading, and talked. "That's just what Buck was afraid of, too. Why, he made me get horses and come the back way while he walked right in here.

I can't imagine what made him do it, because he wasn't a fool." Red glanced down toward the old gray wrinkled face, and with slow shake of head, said, "God, but I feel lonesome."

Then there was a clattering bustle near the rear of the saloon, vague jubilant cries, and a high-pitched voice sang out, "They got him! They got him! Here's Hamel!"

There was a surge of the crowd. Townsmen and cowpunchers milled about Hamel as he was dragged along with a man at each arm. A buzzing babel of questions went up. Hamel was coatless, bareheaded, looked half dazed, and was bleeding from a scalp gash along the side of his head. His holster was empty. His clothes were covered with dirt. The heavy fat jaws quivered, trembling. His little close-set dark eyes bulged in a glazed stare. He mumbled with dry mouth and husky voice, "I ain't done nothing—nothing. Whisky."

He was shoved up in front of Morgan, and men stepped back, leaving a narrow circle. He was a pitiful thing, but there was no pity in the eyes of any man. The rangy, bow-legged, sun-blackened young puncher pushed forward and held out a gun, butt first, to Morgan, saying, "This here's his gun, Mr. Morgan. We found it in the alley. It ain't even been fired—once!"

Sneers ran over the lips of the crowd. Hamel was down now and doomed. The townsmen who had toadied or stood aloof, fearing him, now showed their true feelings scornfully. His men had stood and fought it out and died; but Hamel, with gun unfired, had run. He was yellow to the heart's core. Whimpering in Morgan's face, he said, "We've always been friends, ain't we, Mr. Morgan?"

Morgan ignored him. He looked toward his young sun-blackened puncher and asked quietly, "What happened, Joe? Where'd you find 'im?"

"Well, you see, Mr. Morgan, he was laying out there in the alley. The boys thought at first he was dead, but from what we can guess Hamel must have sneaked out the back way, meaning to bolt, and seen that horse and climbed him—or tried o. That Hellbender. I reckon it was dark and Hamel didn't notice that he was about to get a-straddle of some dynamite wrapped 'round with horsehide."

Red muttered almost inaudibly, "Buck, old man, you made me bring that horse." Then musingly he added, feeling sort of relieved and happy, "And I reckon right now you're leaning over heaven's rail, grinning at Hamel."

"I want to see Monroe," said Hamel, gasping and with a pop-eyed pleading look into Morgan's hard-set face. "I'm sick. I been bad hurt, internal. Men have lied about me to Monroe."

Red spoke up, feeling dry-mouthed, but angry. "Mr. Morgan, take him up to Mr. Monroe, won't you? Old Bill's up there, with his feet and fingers burned. Hamel done it. Shorty Crawley's up there, having blabbed all he knows. Them gamblers are up there, dead, and Monroe knows why they came. Hamel sent 'em. Take him up."

At that, Hamel turned and bucked the crowd, struggling to get through, to get away. He struggled, weak-kneed, letting himself fall, and was held up by the men who had seized him. One moment blasphemy swept across his tongue, the next he was mumbling a frantic prayer.

Disgust, like an expression of pain, came over the faces of men. They were used to seeing even blackguards take it like men. Hamel, the bully, showed himself rotten clear through.

Men dragged him stumblingly along, out the door, into the street, and with surging steps that sent up dust, yanked him along. The crowd went, too, with much running this way and that, some going on ahead to be among the first at the hotel, others milling about to get a better look at Hamel.

Red felt a tug at his arm and heard a voice ask, "Ain't you coming?"

"No," he said, answering before he saw who had spoken. Then he looked into the face of the man named Martin who owned the General Store where Red had bought all his finery and unfortunately had met Harry Stow.

"Say, you—" Red's hand shot out, clutching Martin's arm—"I want my old duds back. Boots—where'd you put 'em?" Then with ideas crowding fast: "Is it you that handles the mail?"

Martin, startled, tried to draw away. He thought Red must be a little out of his head. "No, it's Bob, my clerk."

"Where is he?"

"In the crowd somewheres."

"Listen, I'm going up there, too—you and me—and find that clerk."

CHAPTER 20.

Toward the Cottonwood

Everybody in town tried to crowd into the room where Monroe lay, or into the hall, or on the stairs. All were orderly, for the most part silent, speaking in whispers, waiting.

The crowd willingly, but with difficulty, made way for Morgan as he pushed his way up the stairs, followed by those who were bringing Hamel. At a word, his men stopped with Hamel outside Monroe's room.

Morgan went in, men giving way before him. He stood at the side of the bed, looked into Monroe's uplifted face, then in silence put out his hand.

Monroe, leaning on an elbow, in silence took it.

Years and years before they had been friends. Now, with no word spoken, but with mutual understanding, they had become friends again.

Morgan looked about. He spoke, quietly but with meaning. "Get out, everybody."

Men stirred, shifting their feet, edging toward the door, going backward.

"Take him along," said Morgan, pointing toward Shorty Crawley, still tied, hands and feet.

Crawley was pulled out, carried. Then Morgan closed the door. He and Monroe were alone.

Morgan cleared his throat but said nothing. Monroe coughed. They looked at each other.

"Your boy's out to my place," said Morgan. "He stood the ride fine."

"I want a buckboard fixed up with a mattress on some hay. I'm going out to see him. Be a long time before I can set a saddle again. Maybe never."

"Mrs. Morgan and Margie and me'll be a heap glad to have you visiting us again, Jerry."

"I'll sure be glad to be there again, Oliver."

Morgan cleared his throat some more, fumbled with his belt buckle, pulled at the collar of his shirt, and wiped his face with his neckerchief. He swallowed two or three times, coughed again, then managed to say, "We got Hamel outside here. I thought maybe you'd like to ask him a little something."

Monroe, too, swallowed two or three times, stared blankly at the window, and shook his head.

"No. My boy's come back to me. I'm not going to insult men like the Waxman boys by even listening to Hamel admit he lied about Diamond Jack O'Brien. As for her—Oliver, I hope I roast in hell a long, long time for the way I treated her."

227

Oliver Morgan put out his hand again. Monroe took it. The handshake was long and firm, with no word spoken.

Then Morgan put on his hat, stepped back, and turned toward the door. "I'll be back in about a half hour, Jerry. It won't take long."

"See that my door is kept closed, Oliver. I don't want to see anybody for a spell."

Morgan stepped outside, closing the door behind him. Men, holding their breath, searched his face expectantly. He paused, looked about, then spoke in a calm, low voice to his rangy young puncher. "All right, Joe. Get on with what's got to be done."

"Yessir, Mr. Morgan."

"Everybody clear out. Plumb out of the hall. Go along."

Low words were passed, reaching the people on the stairs and at the foot of the stairs; and the crowd gave way and moved out of the hotel, swarmed on the porch, and clustered in the street. In silence the men who held Hamel pulled him along.

"Mrs. Wyman," said Morgan as he passed her at the foot of the stairs, "Mr. Monroe doesn't want for to see anybody for a spell."

As the crowd thinned on the hotel porch, Red let go of the arm of a thin pimply faced young man, saying, "Scat, you! And consider yourself lucky that it wasn't needful for me to tell how you monkeyed with other folks' mail."

One of Morgan's punchers came riding up,

leading a half dozen horses. Men mounted and sat motionless, waiting. The crowd stood silent, staring. Hamel's hands were tied behind him. Terror seemed to have struck him dumb and left him too weak to struggle. He was lifted bodily into a saddle. Men even fitted his feet into the stirrups.

From his own saddle Morgan loosened the lariat, ran it through his hands, fixed a small loop, and with a quick easy toss set it about Hamel's neck. Then Morgan, not looking at any one, swung into the saddle, let the rope hang loose in his hand and started his horse at a walk. The horse Hamel was on followed at a walk. Behind him rode four other men, at a walk, with hands resting on the horns of their saddles and looking neither to the right nor the left.

They turned left on the main street, going at a walk toward the big cottonwood about a half mile from town.

CHAPTER 21.

Red Rides On—

Late that afternoon Red Clark rode out of Tajola, alone. He rode Hellbender and led his own horse that carried a new blanket roll, tarpaulin, and some camping pans. His saddlebags were stuffed with bacon, beans, and flour, coffee and sugar. Plenty of sugar. Old Bill had asked him to stay on. Mr. Monroe had asked him to stay on. Oliver Morgan had said Mrs. Morgan and Margie both had told him to be sure to give Red a job on his ranch.

But Red had shaken his head stubbornly, saying little. "Nope, after I see old Buck put away, I'm riding. I don't want to stay in this country. Where I'm going I don't know."

Monroe had given him money and confirmed the order on the General Store, sending word that Red was to have whatever he wanted.

Red's first want was his old boots. After that, now having two horses, he bought a bed roll and tarp.

He was riding out and not paying much attention to the direction in which he was going, when he chanced to look up, and there before him at the bend in the road was Hamel's body, dangling motionless at the end of a rope. Red stared at the lumpish form, nodded grimly, then leaned forward and gently patted the neck of Hellbender.

CHAPTER 22.

—And Finds a Friend

Some months later Red came at a lope through the sagebrush and flung himself off, all sweaty and dusty; at the end of a roundup chuckwagon. Horses were all about and strange men from various outfits.

Somebody hit Red on the back, spun him about,

and wrapped an arm about his neck, cussing him affectionately.

"Well, I'll be gosh-darned danged!" Red spluttered jubilantly. "If it ain't Harry Stow. Well, you old wall-eyed lizard, you."

"Yeah," said Stow, backing off and frowning. "You and me are enemies for life. You sure as hell ruined my life."

"Nobody could do as much harm to you as you damn near done to me in Tajola some time back."

"That's just it. You're gazing at a broken-down, hopeless feller who's all spoiled and won't ever be able to eat hearty again. 'Member that there red-headed kid who got shot through the window instead of you?"

"Sort of," Red admitted.

"Well, sir, he came out to our ranch, got all cured, and Margie Morgan up and married him. The next day I took my busted heart in hand and lit out. Red, you sure as hell let yourself in for a lot of disappointment if you work on a ranch where there's a pretty girl. From now on, I'm riding only for bachelors. But say, I got one satisfaction, sure."

"Yeah?"

"Yeah. Margie may've married him, but she keeps telling him there ain't a man in the whole Tajola country who can hold a candle to the riding, fighting, good-looking old Red Clark of Tulluco. He won't get an overdose of happiness out of his married life with her having affectionate memories of your black eyes. Yessir, I bet her first kid, even if it's a girl, will be named Red Clark of Tulluco."

Thereupon Red tripped Harry Stow, and they went rolling about in the sagebrush and sand, happy as two bear cubs at play. Red came up on top, put his knees on Harry's arms, pinning him tight, tickled him in the ribs to help him wiggle, and sprinkled sand on his mouth to teach him not to tell lies about folks, particularly about pretty girls who had the good sense not to marry him. After which they ate some three pounds apiece of steak and hot biscuits, then curled up in blankets, elbow to elbow, smoked cigarettes, and talked far into the bright starlit night.

Center Point Large Print
600 Brooks Road / PO Box 1
Thorndike, ME 04986-0001 USA

(207) 568-3717

US & Canada:
1 800 929-9108
www.centerpointlargeprint.com